Deathless Aphrodite, throned in flowers,
Daughter of Zeus, O terrible enchantress,
With this sorrow, with this anguish, break my spirit,
    Lady, no longer!

Come again to me! O now! Release me!
End the great pang! And all my heart desireth
Now of fulfillment, fulfill! O Aphrodite,
    Fight by my shoulder!

                  —Sappho
                    Mytilene, 610 B.C.

FUGITIVE IN TRANSIT

EDWARD LLEWELLYN

DAW Books, Inc.

Donald A. Wollheim, Publisher

1633 Broadway, New York, N.Y. 10019

PUBLISHED BY
THE NEW AMERICAN LIBRARY
OF CANADA LIMITED

DAW Collectors' Book No. 614

First Printing, February 1985

2 3 4 5 6 7 8 9

PRINTED IN CANADA
COVER PRINTED IN U.S.A.

I

"That's not a fugitive!" The Director of Unipol stared at the picture on his desk. "That's a woman."

"It looks like a woman," said the Galactic Marshal. "I look like a man. I am not a man. But, when properly clothed, most humans will accept me as human."

The Director looked at his visitor and feared that was true. The last Galactic Marshal (the title was the invention of some journalist) to visit Unipol Headquarters had left looking like a composite of all the males on the staff; it had still been thinking like an alien. Now he had another Marshal inflicted on him, together with a request from the Director-General of the

United Nations to give it whatever help it demanded. Which apparently meant helping it capture some off-world crook who looked like a woman.

He resumed his inspection of the fugitive's picture. A flat card, a piece of alien gadgetry, which gave a three-dimensional image when placed under a light, so that the small figure on it seemed to stand smiling up at him. A figure which looked like a woman, and a beautiful woman at that. It might look like something else without its clothes. Or it might not.

"The English approximation to its name is 'Alia'," said the Marshal.

"And it's a mimic like you?"

"A mimic certainly, but not like me."

"Then it used a woman as its model?"

"I was pursuing Alia long before anybody knew humans existed."

"We always knew we existed!" snapped the Director.

The Marshal amended his statement and increased the insult. "Before we knew you existed."

"You mean you've been chasing this crook for more than twenty years?"

"For much longer than twenty years. From before humans burst into the Transits."

The Director frowned, remembering the summer when humans had discovered they were not potential lords of the universe but only high-tech barbarians. Barbarians who had blundered into Spiral Arm civilization and been welcomed with resignation rather than warmth.

The summer when the energy shortage in North America had become as critical as the food shortages in Asia and Africa. Private homes in many American cities had had to forgo air-conditioning, and public anger had forced the Federal Government to goad research teams toward finding new sources of energy. A team on a University of California campus had achieved a burst of fusion great enough to break through into a Transit channel.

A channel's boundaries are self-sealing but during the few seconds of rupture everything movable on campus had been sucked into it. Subjective seconds later an unscheduled shipment had arrived at the next Transit junction. Accidental invasion of a Transit is rare, but the junction operators are trained to deal with such emergencies. They had recognized members of an oxygen-breathing race, extracted them from the inanimate debris, and shipped them to the nearest vacant oxygen world.

Normally they would have been left there to populate a fertile but unused planet and, if capable, to develop a society worthy of acceptance into civilization. But when investigation showed that the incident was not due to accident but caused by the intruders themselves the Auld were faced with the likelihood of further intrusions. Earth was the paradoxical combination of high-level technology and low-level sociology, likely to autodestruct in the near future. Those races with a taste for obscene humor called Earth a self-solving problem.

The Auld, who dominate the Transit Authority, have no noticeable sense of humor but an imperative sense of responsibility. The welfare of the several thousand worlds served by the Transits depends on the integrity of the system, and they could not risk damage to even one section while waiting for the human problem to solve itself. They drove a pilot channel through to Earth and sent in a survey team.

The shaft emerged in Bengal where the third major famine in six years had coincided with a cholera epidemic. The team assumed this was the aftermath of some unique natural disaster, but the only functioning beings they found during their first reconnaissance were a Doctor Bose and his helpers. Minutes later there was only Doctor Bose; his helpers had taken one look at the blue-gowned strangers and left. Bose, then a young physician, semi-delirious from fever and exhaustion, had hardly noticed the appearance of their replacements. He had handed the first Auld to arrive an infusion kit with orders to hold it while he set up a peritoneal infusion on a dehydrated infant. Then he had moved to the next child, telling his helper to fetch him another kit.

He had glanced at his new assistants occasionally as he went from infant to infant, child to child, adult to adult. They had seemed as human as the living skeletons or bloated bags he was trying to keep alive. When the strangers had begun to distribute food from somewhere he had blessed them for a rare humanity.

The Auld's first attempt at Terran food had been a nourishing mess; the second a kind of ersatz rice. Thereafter the shipments had improved to an imitation rice of a better quality than most of the starving had ever eaten, handed out freely to all who came to collect. Once the Transit was in full operation it was the dealers' trucks which had come, followed closely by Government officials. The trucks had disappeared in the direction of private godowns and Government grainaries. The Transit Terminal had been surrounded by rioting mobs. The Transit Guard had demonstrated, by rescuing merchants and officials from the mob's claws, that a single armed Auld could stun humans by the thousand. And the Guard's discovery that the humans they rescued were fat whereas those they had to stun were thin, brought home to them the horror of the situation.

Bose had glanced at the fracas occasionally while continuing to salvage men, women, and children, sending his helpers off to fetch him more patients, drugs, and infusion kits. The patients they brought remained the same human wreckage but the drugs and infusion kits became unfamiliar. His helpers also changed from gowned strangers to helmeted, masked, and armed figures in loose coveralls. The Auld had switched to operational gear when the rioting started. Bose assumed they were riot police.

He had been hallucinating on and off for days. When soldiers arrived and the shooting began his assistant had pushed him to the ground and lain on top of him. He had noted with interested disbelief that the coveralls seemed impervious to bullets. After that episode he had returned to his task only pausing to watch, with the detached amusement of a dreamer who knows he is dreaming, his assistant draw a side-arm and knock out a squadron of tanks. Later, he had hardly looked up when another helper had swatted a swarm of buzzing aircraft. Oscillating between fatigue and exhaustion, between reality and hallucination, Doctor Bose had continued to rehydrate babies.

He had only collapsed when they had told him gently that all his remaining patients were dead. By this time the Auld had decided that Doctor Bose was the only sane being in a demented world and they treated him with the care due a rare specimen. Days later, when consciousness filtered back, he had found himself discussing with his dream-images what should be done to change the hell of the present into the heaven of the future.

He knew that he was hallucinating, that these people must be creations of his subconscious, because nobody else had ever shared his hopes for mankind nor his conviction that the United Nations was the way to salvation. That, he explained, was why he worked for the World Health Organization. His dream-people had listened and asked for his advice. He had given it at length. The Auld, finding themselves saddled with the immediate well-being of humanity and unable to contact any other human who talked sense, started to put their ethical imperatives into effect along the lines that Bose suggested.

For the pragmatic Auld taking responsibility meant taking control. One side-arm on full power could slice up a suburb, sink an aircraft carrier, or reflect a nuclear explosion. They preferred to stun rather than kill and after their initial show of force it was usually enough to stun. The cobbled-together Terran League fell apart as its demoralized troops reverted to banditry or revolution.

The Auld, following Bose's idealistic advice,

ignored governments and recognized only the United Nations. The Director-General, the new title imposed on the Secretary General, was a mild Japanese lepidopterist who found himself signing a treaty on behalf of Earth. Shortly afterwards the Californians, whom everyone assumed had been swallowed by the San Andreas fault, arrived back via a direct Transit channel. Some of them stayed only long enough to collect the equipment they needed for exploiting the riches of what they called New California, later renamed Nuerth by the other humans who had flooded after them.

Before national governments had recovered a measure of control over their peoples, the Transit Authority had opened up branch terminals all over Earth and begun to meet the obvious shortages. The Transits did more than provide fast and easy transport between civilized worlds, they tapped the tremendous centrifugal forces of a rotating galaxy to provide almost unlimited electrical power to the worlds they served.

By the time humans realized that they were not even aspirants to Arm civilization, the Transits were restoring electrical affluence to Europe and North America, and raising famine to mere starvation elsewhere on Earth. The Transit between Nuerth and the mother-planet began to relieve population pressures almost immediately and now, twenty years later, was turning comfort into luxury. The Transit Authority had an eon-old tradition of open access to the system for all civilized individuals. Humans were not civilized and were therefore confined to the Transit leading to Nuerth, but the Authority was adamant in assuring them equal access to that. It became almost impossible for an unwanted tyrant to survive in the face of mass emigration.

By enforcing a relative calm the Auld saved hundreds of millions from physical suffering. Terran leaders insisted they had caused a vast amount of psychological suffering by demeaning the human self-image. Speakers in the General Assembly demanded that Earth be left to solve its problems in its own way, and especially the problem of law and order on Nuerth, which should be divided so that the have-not nations could attain territorial equality with the haves. Moreover, many of the Transit Terminals on both worlds had been sited without regard to human wishes and administrative needs. They must be closed.

Members of the Transit Authority had listened incredulously to the debate and then pointed out that closing Terminals would lead to local hardships. Representatives of various governments had answered that those hardships were not comparable to the disorganization and conflicts caused by alien territorial encroachments.

Once the Auld had made sure they understood what the speakers were saying they had thereafter ignored the General Assembly and communicated only with the Director-General. They shared his fascination with nature and he seemed rational. They had made his word the law. If his orders were not obeyed then the electrical power supplied by the Transits was reduced step-by-step in the rebellious areas; usually even the most bellicose lost their ardor as their amenities shrank. The world lived under the rule of a man originally selected because of his genius for compromise. Basically a good man, he got the Auld blamed for some of the good he ordered. A request from the DG now had the force of a command, to be resented but obeyed.

The Director returned his attention from past disillusionment to the present problem. The more he studied the image of Alia the greater the problem became. "Does she—it—really look like this?"

"I have met Alia, and I can confirm that image is an excellent likeness."

"If the public sees this it won't be easy to persuade them that she's an alien."

"Very few should see it, and even fewer know what it is. I am aware that the spectacle of a Galactic Marshal, the absurd name given us by your news media, carrying off a creature that looks like a woman would cause disturbances."

"Disturbances? There'd be mobs trying to smash the Transits! Human beings lose all sense of proportion—" The Director checked himself. "Have you told anybody else about its arrival?"

"I have told nobody on Earth except yourself, not even our own Embassy."

"Isn't that rather—?"

"I outrank the incumbent ambassadors by many levels. There is only one other human who must know. The Deputy who acts as liaison officer between our embassy and the Director-General's office. His name is Doctor Bose."

"I have already asked Doctor Bose to attend our meeting. But before I invite him to join us, how can Unipol help? Our techniques—"

"Your techniques are suited to your society. I wish to arrest Alia without arousing comment. So it must be seized by human police, then handed over to me for transportation from Earth. As it is not a native of Earth it is under my jurisdiction. That is clearly stated in the treaty."

"But—" The Director again stared at the image. "But if she is a woman then the treaty—"

"Any offender against Transit law is under my jurisdiction. There have not as yet been any human offenders. Because human movements are restricted to journeys between Earth and Nuerth no human has had the opportunity to break Transit law. I mention this only to emphasize that, under the Treaty, I have the authority to arrest and transport Alia wherever he, she, or it originates. As I have the authority to demand aid and obedience from all Terran organizations and individuals. I would prefer not to have to assert my authority openly. I hope you agree with that, Director?"

"I do indeed!" The less he knew about what this pair of aliens was up to the better. "You can trust my discretion absolutely. However there is one problem—"

"Yes?"

"None of us here at Unipol Headquarters is experienced in police work. I must ask you to appreciate that we are more—well—diplomats."

"I appreciate that the United Nations and its organizations are still, after twenty years, the creatures of your national governments. And that UN officials are chosen for their ability to compromise rather than to act. Nobody whose appointment depends upon agreement between many groups with conflicting interests is likely to be a resolute character."

The Director flushed. "My only power is that of persuasion."

"On the contrary, in this operation you have great power, should you wish to use it. You have but to mention to me the name of any authority who fails to meet your requests and I will start reducing the supply of electrical energy to that area. The supply of food and raw materials too, if need be."

"For God's sake! Don't even—"

"It will not come to that. Our Ambassadors have already passed the message on. You will be surprised at the alacrity with which your requests are met." The Marshal paused to let the Director consider the warning. "Now, if Doctor Bose is available, I would like to meet him."

"Of course," said the Director, thankful that he would not have to continue facing this implacable alien alone.

Doctor Bose stood looking across New York City from his office high in the UN Tower, awaiting a call for help from the Director of Unipol, ten floors below. The Director had phoned to say an Auld official was visiting him that morning, probably with some incomprehensible complaint, and would Alec Bose come down and give him a hand. In his role as Deputy Director-General with special responsibility for alien relations Bose was continually being called upon to help some UN official understand what the Auld were demanding, and then to explain to the aliens why it couldn't be done.

Every year Doctor Bose asked to be returned to World Health, and every year his request was rejected. The DG had no other Deputy able to advise him so well on alien attitudes and, while UN officials distrusted anyone who could establish rapport with the Auld, they knew they would soon be in trouble without his aid. They asked him to pacify the aliens while calling him "alien-lover" behind his back. Had they known the full story of his first contact they would have condemned him as a traitor to humanity.

He had considered himself as such when, twenty years before, he had recovered sufficiently to realize he had been advising not dream-images of his own creation but aliens who had invaded Earth. He had stayed in their care until he was strong enough to travel, and by then he had learned more about them than any other human being had learned since.

He had begged them to keep their discussions with him secret. They had not properly understood why he wanted this, but had finally agreed not to betray him to his fellows and had allowed him to return to his real task, that of treating the victims of plague and famine. By then the short conflict between the

Terran League and the Transit Authority was over and the chaotic aftermath was providing plenty of both.

The World Health Organization was more accustomed and better equipped to function under conditions of chaos than most bodies. When he reached the Asian headquarters of WHO in New Delhi nobody asked him where he had been. They gave him a team and sent him off to tackle another cholera epidemic. This had again brought him into contact with the Auld and his seniors had noted his success in obtaining help and supplies from the aliens. In due course he had been pulled back first to New Delhi, then to New York, to act as alien liaison officer. Finally he had been promoted to Deputy Director-General, a specialist in the kind of thankless task he was about to face.

Doctor Bose's success in translating human wishes into Auld terms and vice versa was not due to that first contact alone. He had been desensitized to xenophobia as a child by his exposure to four varieties of stranger-hatred. His full name was Alexander Selin Tanaka Bose, and his names represented his genes. He was a mixture of four races, four religions, and four life-styles. His parents had died trying to contain an outbreak of plague with an ineffective vaccine. He had become the joint ward of four feuding grandparents; grandparents whose own interracial marriages had failed and who had been infuriated to see their childrens' succeed.

Each grandparent had claimed him for a quarter of the year and each had considered the customs of the other three to be savage, obscene, or absurd. He had grown up rotating through four major varieties of intolerance, a kind of universal alien, better equipped emotionally and intellectually to meet a real alien than most other human beings. He would rather have been fighting epidemic diseases in the tropics than trying to cope with the xenophobia endemic in the United Nations, but the Puritan sense of duty inherited from his atheist parents, the idealism they had shown in their deaths, kept him acting the buffer between resentful humans and impassive Auld.

The telephone rang and his secretary said, "The Director of Unipol's visitor has arrived. They're waiting for you now, Doctor."

He turned from the window. "Thank you, Miss Forbes. Please tell the Director I'm on my way." A shortish brown-skinned man with thinning hair and a thickening waist, old-fashioned in his manners and many of his beliefs, he took his staff into his confidence and treated them with courtesy; a modest man, he never realized how much they admired him.

In the elevator he braced himself to deal

with the animosity which had probably already developed between the Director of Unipol and his visitor. Alien etiquette was often the antithesis of human courtesy and humans tended to insult any alien they met, sometimes by intention but more often by conduct the Auld judged uncivilized. Bose, who had spent his boyhood switching from fingers, to chopsticks, to forks, had learned enough of Auld manners to avoid direct insults. When he entered the Director's office he ignored the Director and faced the figure by the window. "I am Alexander Selin Tanaka Bose!" For some reason the Auld seemed impressed by his having four names.

"Doctor Bose—" the Director was starting to say when he was silenced by a peremptory gesture from the Marshal, who had risen to his feet.

"I am Sludic." The alien's voice was as firm and regular as his features. His hair was short and blond, his body lean and tall. He gave an impression of strength and authority; an impression his mimicry was designed to give, but which also reflected the truth. The Marshals were Auld of considerable physical strength and a great deal of authority. "I have been on Earth five days."

In accepting Bose's offer to exchange names the Marshal was making a gesture of trust.

Among the Auld, as in many human cultures, when you gave a new acquaintance your name you gave him some claim upon you. Bose allowed a decent interval for mutual contemplation, then asked, "For what purpose?"

Sludic paused for a somewhat shorter interval. "To capture a fugitive."

"You seek a fugitive. Who is that fugitive?"

"Its name is Alia."

"What is its offence?"

"That is no concern of yours."

This curt exchange was the Auld equivalent of an informal chat. Humans found such abruptness insulting, and thereafter most conversations between humans and Auld deteriorated into formality and misunderstanding. But Bose was relieved to have established communication so quickly and to find that the Marshal was speaking fluent English. Most Auld spoke English the way a German speaks French.

"What is the fugitive's species?" Bose asked. To his knowledge there were over eight thousand aliens from some sixty different species scattered around Earth. All were under direct Auld supervision and none spoke any Earth language. Most were physically unattractive, some were frankly repulsive, and all avoided human efforts to make contact. The Transit Administration described the visitors as the equivalent of social scientists from various parts of the Arm recording the details of a native culture before it was eroded by contact with civilization. The methodology of their disciplines demanded the aloofness of the scientific observer from the phenomenon being observed.

"I do not know Alia's species."

Bose allowed himself a click of surprise. The Auld rarely admitted their ignorance of anything. If faced with a question they could not or did not wish to answer, they said nothing. Nobody had yet caught an Auld in a direct lie, but sometimes they used silence to mislead. "Is this fugitive on Earth?"

"Yes."

"Where on Earth?"

"I do not know."

For an Auld to admit ignorance twice within two exchanges indicated a degree of intimacy Bose had not reached since the days when he had been fighting famine and cholera alongside them. It also suggested that Sludic was of high status for it meant that he was working alone. The Auld usually worked in groups, or at least in pairs. "And you are seeking human aid in your search for Alia?"

"I require the full cooperation of all Terran authorities. I am expecting the Terran police to discover its whereabouts and make the arrest. I will then take custody and remove it from Earth. The Marshal picked up the picture from the Director's desk and handed it to Bose. "That is its present appearance."

Bose did not allow his face to show surprise. He had found that the Auld, like his samurai grandfather, favored an inscrutable response to the unexpected, and that when he had pushed an infusion kit into the hands of the first Auld he had met with orders to hold it, his single-minded semiconscious action had given him instant status. So he studied the picture without expression and then asked, "Do you wish copies of this circulated to all security authorities with orders to arrest if seen?"

"No. I wish as few humans as possible to see that original picture."

"Will you wish it to be computer-matched against all the pictures in Unipol's records? Those records include a large proportion of living Caucasians."

"That would be acceptable as an initial step."

"If you do not want it known that this—this individual is an alien, the search must be in terms of a Terran female criminal. What charges shall I name against it?"

The Marshal said nothing. He was not going to make himself a party to deception; that was to be a Terran responsibility.

Bose understood the Marshal's silence. "Then initially we can only ask Unipol to match for a face. If a match is identified the individual can be found by routine police methods and surveillance instituted. The police will then inform you where and who she is in her human guise and, with your approval, make arrangements for her arrest and interrogation."

"No arrest must be made without my direct order. I wish to be kept constantly informed of the progress of the search. I will also wish to meet those police officers who have to be shown Alia's picture."

"The Director of Unipol will doubtless arrange that officers from the appropriate police forces are assigned specifically to this operation."

"I wish them to be assigned specifically to you, Doctor Bose. I wish you, personally, to be in charge of the operation."

"Sludic, I am a Deputy Director-General and have neither experience in nor responsibility for police operations."

"Doctor Bose, the Director-General, at my request, is assigning you to cooperate with me in the search for and the arrest of Alia."

For the first time since he had entered the room Bose looked at the flabbergasted Director of Unipol. "You have heard what has been said. I have no wish to become a policeman, but I have to obey the DG's orders. I will inform you when I require experienced police officers to aid me. In the meantime I will have a standard photograph of this picture prepared and sent to you for Unipol computer search and identification. Give it the highest priority."

"If that's what the Marshal wants—" the infuriated Director started to say.

"That is my wish." The Marshal moved toward the door. "Contact me only through Doctor Bose. Remember this search must remain absolutely secret and that the penalties for failure will be severe." Then, signaling Bose to follow, he walked out of the office. The Doctor paused in the doorway to give the Director an apologetic smile and was rewarded with an angry glare. Overtaking Sludic in the corridor, he said, "Please understand, I have no real power. I am only a figurehead."

"You have proved an excellent interpreter."

"I interface between the Transit Authority and the Director-General."

"My English is still imperfect. So tell me how a figurehead can interface?" When Bose gave a helpless gesture, the Marshal continued. "I do not wish to have any visible contact with our Embassy or with the Transit Authority. I therefore require some human habitation."

"Are you alone?"

"You might not expect it, but I am alone."

Bose had not expected it. To find secure accommodation for an individual Auld of high rank who was unfamiliar with Earth was another alien problem dumped on him. He hesitated, then said, "I am also alone. I have a large apartment near this building. Would you care to stay with me for the time being?"

The Marshal considered this novel suggestion. No Auld had ever shared accommodation with a human. "Yes. Then you will be able to explain human behavior to me."

"That I cannot promise, Sludic. I don't understand it myself. But I'll try to describe it."

II

Peter Ward had left the village an hour before dawn, intending to reach the ruins of the temple fifteen minutes before sunrise. But the path was longer and steeper than he remembered and the two surviving pillars of Aphrodite's ancient shrine were already silhouetted against the lightening sky when he scrambled over the rocky ridge above the promontory. This was the morning when the Pleiades rose with the sun, the ancient starsign that the season for seafaring and farming had arrived. He had come to watch the rising from Aphrodite's temple, and had barely reached the ridge in time. He was about to clamber down the slope to the ruins when he saw a woman standing between the pillars.

He had planned to watch from where she stood, but he did not relish the company of some female tourist. So he stayed on the ridge, taking a bearing from the grass-covered mounds which marked the line of the temple walls. A glow on the horizon showed where the sun was about to rise from the sea, and he searched among the paling constellations for the Daughters of Atlas.

In an appendix to his doctoral thesis, "The Siting of Doric Temples," Peter Ward had speculated that there might be a relationship between the stars sacred to a goddess and the orientation of her shrines. As a young scholar in a field almost devoid of young scholars and with a consequent lack of competition for travel funds, he had been able to get regular grants which allowed him to leave Cornell every spring and fall to spend several weeks in Greece testing his hypothesis. Weeks of escape from a detestable present to a mythical past, from an upper New York State vulgarized by the affluence of cheap power and Arm trade to Greek hillsides barren from goats, overfarming, and lost populations.

Few tourists came to Psara this early in the year, and fewer still climbed to these remote ruins. Most Classics scholars were now too old to climb anything but library stairs. Peter had come to regard these places as his own, and he resented having to share this dawn with a stranger.

He found the first ghost-star of the Pleiades just above the horizon, and then studied the silhouette of the intruder. A female silhouette with a figure that was no insult to Aphrodite. In the dawn light he could not tell the color or details of her clothes, but she seemed to be wearing one of the fashionable bodyfitting jumpsuits. Since she was standing with her back toward him as she looked out toward the sunrise, he could not see her face, and her hair was caught up in a scarf, but her stance gave an impression of youth and restrained energy. Reluctantly he shifted his attention to the scarlet glow on the horizon; the point from which Helios was about to send his three-horsed chariot galloping across the Heavens.

The glow became a crescent arc, the first brilliant ray flashed up into the deep blue of the dawn sky. The woman lifted onto her toes, raised her arms toward the rising sun, and began to sing.

Peter caught his breath as he recognized the song. She was singing Sappho's Ode to Aphrodite, one of the few surviving works of the woman whom the Greeks had called "The Tenth Muse," the greatest lyric poet who had ever lived. And she was singing in the original

Aeolic dialect; the pre-classical Greek of these islands.

Her accent was unorthodox but matched the words, and her stresses showed she understood the meaning of the song. She gave the sapphics the inflections which brought life to the lines, letting them swoop and rise, vibrate again with Sappho's own passionate adoration of beauty. The passion which had entranced listeners two thousand six hundred years before entranced Peter Ward. As she finished the last stanza he stood up to applaud, but she continued to sing.

In the whole world there were few scholars who combined a knowledge of Aeolic Greek with an ear sensitive enough to judge a poem heard for the first time. A bad poem need be heard only once to be recognized as bad, but to separate the mediocre from the good requires sufficient repetitions to detect false phrases or appreciate subtle beauties. To Peter, at first hearing, the verses added by some unknown author sounded as beautiful as the earlier lines written by Sappho herself.

The woman finished the ode and dropped her arms. Peter started down the slope, eager to introduce himself as a fellow scholar and find the source of the last stanza. He had slid only a short way when he froze, awestruck.

The woman had jerked off her scarf, letting her hair tumble free to her shoulders. The rays of the rising sun turned it to a flowing halo, a brilliant auburn-golden nimbus.

The intrusion of Arm civilization had ended many human dreams. It had forced vast rearrangements upon human religions and philosophies. During the twenty years since the arrival of the Auld, religious leaders and abstract philosophers had learned how to cope with the new image of the cosmos as they had learned to cope with earlier intellectual upheavals. Pragmatists, materialists, and scientists had altered the direction of their respective searches for power, profits, or knowledge but had not greatly changed their styles. By now the vast majority of human beings had readjusted to the new place of humanity in the natural order at least as effectively as the Japanese had readjusted to Perry's arrival at Edo Bay. And, as in Japan, the group hit hardest by the impact of an alien civilization had been the romantics.

The majority of romantics had become activists, throwing the energies of their frustrations into polemics and, less often, physical protests; trying to mobilize the mass of their fellow-humans into a crusade to liberate Earth from the Auld yoke. A minority had tried to ignore the alien presence by continuing to pursue romanticism through fantasy, art, and scholarship.

Peter Ward was a poet by talent, a scholar by avocation. Early in his college career he had been a hard-core activist, devoting his weekends to the rigorous training the cadre imposed on the young men and women who believed they were learning to become liberators when they were actually being turned into terrorists. The cadre had noted Peter's physical strength, his intelligence, and his romantic enthusiasms. They had seen in him a potential cell leader and given him special training in unarmed combat and underground organization. They had underestimated his common sense. When the unarmed combat evolved into weapon training he had realized he was being groomed to act the assassin; when he had ingested the activist creed he had found only vogue words, vague concepts, and bloody murder. He had eased himself out of the movement.

Unlike most activist drop-outs he had not climbed on the escalator of a booming economy. He had seen no place for his poetic impulse, his love of language, his sense of beauty in the contemporary world and had retreated to the past. He had become a classical scholar, choosing to live among the romantic illusions of heroic times rather than the affluent disillusion of the present. For years he had been steeping himself in Greek myths, and the awe which checked his slide down the ridge was the momentary thought that the glowing figure standing in Aphrodite's temple might be the goddess herself. An absurd thought, but while he hesitated the singer ran from the ruins to the edge of the cliff and, with a leap, disappeared.

She was either a goddess or she'd broken her neck! Peter slid down the scree amid an avalanche of small stones, picked himself up, and raced to the spot where she had vanished. Peering over the edge, he saw she had neither flung herself to her death nor taken off for Olympus. She was leaping from rock to rock on her way down the cliff-face, following a goat trail with the agility of a mountaineer.

He watched her reach the track winding along the beach and stared after her as she ran toward the village. When she had disappeared around the headland he decided he was not mountain-climber enough to follow her down, and he walked slowly across the grass to sit on the old stones and organize his thoughts.

She was certainly mortal. A goddess would not have imitated a mountain goat. And her tight blue jumpsuit was the current fashion for women with her figure. She was an athlete, a singer, and one of the few people in the world who could speak Aeolic Greek. It was even deader than classical Greek, a dialect of interest to only a few scholars. He thought he knew them all, at least by reputation. None could claim personal beauty, athletic ability, and the voice of Calypso.

She had disappeared toward the village, and as there was no boat from the island until the next day she must be staying in its only hotel. He got to his feet, took one look down the goat path, and started on the longer but less terrifying route home.

He found her easily enough; she was sitting on the veranda of the hotel eating rolls, drinking coffee, and reading a week-old *New York Times*. She looked up at his "Good morning," responded with a nod, and returned to her newspaper. With her hair in a scarf and her body hidden by a loose kimono it was hard to imagine her as the hymning Aphrodite of dawn.

He went into the hotel to consult the register and the proprietor. Her name was Ruth Adams, she was American, and the only address given was care of American Express, Athens. The proprietor showed him the register with a leer. "That lady—too tough!" Peter thanked him for the information, collected his own breakfast, and returned to the veranda.

He sat down at the next table and remarked to the newspaper. "Lovely morning."

The paper ignored him.

Such a summary rejection would usually have snuffed out Peter's interest. As a large, good-looking, and amiable young man of a romantic disposition and with a poet's skill in the use of words, he obtained an adequate amount of female companionship without having to suffer the pain of rebuffs. But on this occasion he was not trying to pick up a beautiful woman, he was trying to introduce himself to a fellow scholar. During his walk back to the village he had considered his approach and decided that she might not appreciate having been watched from the shadows. So his next remark only hinted at what had happened. "Didn't I see you up at the temple this morning?"

The newspaper dropped, exposing a pair of blazing blue eyes. "What the hell were you doing up there?"

"Watching the sunrise. From up on the ridge. Way back up!" He was scorched by her glare and tried to cool it by explaining his theory. "Today's the heliacal rising of the Pleiades. That means they rise near dawn. In ancient times that was the sign for the planting—"

"You're not a farmer, so what's it to you?" She folded her newspaper and put it on the table beside her. He had roused more than her interest; he was under intense scrutiny. She was demanding an explanation for his presence at the temple. And acting as if she had the right to make such a demand.

"I have a theory—not a very good theory—that the orientation of a temple dedicated to a goddess was related to her particular constellations. Now—"

"You're right. It's not a very good theory!"

Peter's reaction to this cavalier dismissal of his hypothesis was instant resentment. He met her glare for glare. "How do you know? You haven't heard my evidence."

"I don't need to! I know—" She brought herself to a halt, the fire went from her eyes, and her voice softened. "I'm sorry. That was rude of me. I guess I was surprised that anybody's still interested in Greek temples. And your idea is so novel that I—well—just rejected it out of hand. That's what usually happens to new ideas, isn't it? Please forgive me."

"Of course." Her smile would have brought forgiveness for anything. "You're probably right. The evidence is pretty weak. Just strong enough to raise a travel grant!" She rewarded his academic humor with another smile. "Are you in Classics?"

"In Classics?" She was momentarily puzzled, then shook her head. "I gather you are?"

"I teach Classics. Or try to."

"What do you teach?"

"My field's the Greek lyric poets." He waved in the general direction of Lesbos. "Alcaeus, Sappho, et cetera."

"So you're a poet?" She leaned forward.

"Yes—no—not exactly." He had once heard a girl remark, "Poets are pathetic really! They're so obsolete!" Since then he had never mentioned his poetry to a woman. But he could not deny it to her. "I've written some verse. But you can't make a living from poetry."

"He didn't make much of a living either!" She glanced past him toward the island on the horizon.

"You mean Homer? 'The blind poet who lived in rugged Chios?' He didn't have to teach undergraduates. And he did have an audience."

"He still has an audience. He's had an audience for nearly three thousand years. And now it's expanding."

"Expanding? Like hell it is! None of the kids learn Homeric Greek any more. Not even the Greek kids. And not many read Homer in translation."

She shrugged, studied him, and then asked suddenly, "What's your name?"

"Peter Ward."

"I'm Ruth Adams. Ruth Thalia Adams. I prefer to be called Thalia." She held out her hand. He took it, entranced. "Have you visited Psara before?"

"Twice."

She recovered her hand. "Perhaps you'd show me round?"

He jumped to his feet. "Of course!"

"Then sit down and finish your breakfast while I change." And she disappeared into the hotel while Peter subsided into his chair, trying to realign his thoughts as he drank cold coffee.

She returned in her blue jumpsuit, a rucksack on her back, and took Peter's arm as they started up the village street. "Now, Professor, tell me about the history of this little island."

"It was lucky—it hasn't much! That ruin's one of the few interesting places on it. Oh—in antiquity it was supposed to have had an entrance to the underworld hidden somewhere." She seemed to tense, and he looked down at her face. "There were entrances to the underworld all round the Mediterranean."

"There's something fascinating about Hades." She bit her lip. "I mean, to the old Greeks."

As they walked in the brisk morning air she encouraged him to start talking about himself. When he quoted a line from one of his sonnets to illustrate a point she insisted he recite the whole and praised him when he finished. "That's beautiful, Peter! Better than beautiful—it's good."

He laughed. "Some old general advised young men that when a girl appears to enjoy listening to them recite poetry they should be very very careful!"

"It's I who must be careful!" She turned away from him. "Let's climb up there and have lunch."

They ate sitting on the rough grass high above the harbor. He was entirely happy until he glanced toward Chios; a shadow seemed to pass over his mind and he muttered, "The bastards!"

"Who?" She looked sideways at him.

"Those damned aliens who come to study us. What the hell are they after? They're supposed to be scholars, but I've never seen any of their scholarship. The Auld at least make themselves look more or less human and talk English. The others don't even bother to learn our language. A squidgy kind of creature came to the maths department last year. Complete with an Auld escort to translate and protect of course! It seemed to understand what our maths people were saying, but it said damned little back."

"Perhaps it didn't have anything worth saying?"

"Thalia, those people were traveling between the stars when we were living in caves!"

"Nobody travels between stars. They're much too hot!" She laughed, then put her hand on his arm to check his frown. "Do you think they come to study us like we used to study our own aborigines? To record the quaint, disgusting, and primitive habits of societies about to be swamped by civilization? Is that what you think?"

"For them—what else about us is worth studying?" His cynicism was the typical romantic reaction to the alien fact.

"Peter, there's a lot they can learn from us. Especially the Auld." She put her arm round his shoulders and rested her cheek against his. Her hair brushed his lips and her perfume filled his nostrils. A fragrance aromatic rather than sweet; it kindled his imagination and brightened the world around him. "Look down at the harbor. Do you think it's changed much in the last twenty-eight hundred years?"

He shook his head, not wanting to speak, fearing to break the spell.

"Now look toward Chios and use your imagination. Do you see that galley, out there in the distance, rowing toward Psara?"

He imagined such a galley. An instant later he saw it, distant but distinct on the sunlit ocean, trailing a white wake. "Yes, I see it!"

Her lips were at his ear, her voice murmured smoothly on. A galley from Chios, bound for Skiros away to the west. She would put in to Psara to spend the night and perhaps wait for a fair wind to aid her on the long sea-crossing ahead. The words guided him in building an image which became as vivid as the ocean and the rocks.

The galley was about thirty meters long with a beam of four meters and twenty pairs of oars. He could distinguish the two steering oars aft, one to port and one to starboard, with a bearded helmsman standing between, shouting orders, encouragement, and curses at the rowers.

He was aware of Thalia's soft voice, the warmth of her lips, the fragrance of her perfume, the touch of her hair on his cheek. He forgot he was hallucinating as he watched the galley knifing through the swell toward the harbor, as she rolled in the rip across the entrance, as she slid across the smooth waters of the basin. The Master shouted. The starboard oars churned, backing water as the port bank gave way to swing the galley round in the old Achean style, then the sun flashed off forty dripping blades as the rowers shipped their oars. Men on the wharf calling as the galley glided alongside, heaving-lines snaking out, mooring lines bent on, securing the galley to the wharf, riding against inflated goatskin fenders. He watched, fascinated, as a gangplank was run out, as people streamed on and off the ship. A tall man, his beard flecked with gray, rose from under a shelter rigged in the stern and started along the catwalk between the rowers' benches, his hand resting on the shoulder of a youth, a girl coming behind carrying his belongings. Peter watched the youth and the girl guide the bearded man from catwalk to gangplank and from gangplank to wharf.

He had forgotten that this was something conjured up by his own imagination, guided by Thalia's whispered words, and was watching the scene on the wharf when her voice cut into his dream. "What's that? Off shore? Breaking surface. A whale?"

"A sub! A nuclear sub!" The bridge, the planes, the whole sail rose dripping from the sea until the dark length of the hull was awash. Men in uniform emerged onto her bridge as she turned her bows toward the harbor. He was trying to read the number painted on her sail when he saw a White Ensign broken out from the staff at the after end of the bridge.

"A British nuclear sub! What the hell's she doing here?"

There was a flurry of water as her engines went astern, slowing her as she approached the harbor entrance; the spray flew as she shouldered through the rip, then calm as she glided across the basin, losing way until she was hanging motionless a cable length off the wharf. Her officers had binoculars to their eyes as they studied the scene ashore.

The sailors on the galley were shouting and pointing. Some of the crowd turned to look at the new arrival, but most continued to cluster around the bearded man who had taken a kithara from the youth. He paused, his blind eyes looking out to sea, and then struck a chord which went echoing across the harbor so that even the sailors stopped shouting and the crowd fell silent. On the sub the hum of engines died at her captain's signal.

The singer plucked a softer note, and then his voice rolled out in sonorous hexameters, singing of the anger of Achilles before the walls of Troy. The whole harbor was silent save for that voice, as men and women, Peter among them, held their breath and the giant image of the shining Achilles, the truculent, cruel and sensitive hero was conjured up by the blind singer.

The vision started to fade, the singer's voice

moved away into the distance. Crowds, galley, submarine, and singer shimmered and were gone. He was again staring down at the modern village sleeping in the afternoon sun.

He turned to look at her, still dazed. Her eyes were so blue. Lines from a Homeric hymn floated into his mind: "I sing the glorious Goddess with azure eyes,/ Athenian Pallas! Timeless, chaste, and wise." The Goddess was saying, "So you really are a poet!"

"A poet?" She blinded him and he looked toward the sea.

"You have a poet's imagination. I suggested you imagine what the harbor was like long ago, and then picture the reactions of the sailors aboard a Greek galley to the appearance of a nuclear submarine. I meant it to be an analogy to human reactions at the arrival of the Auld. But you went far beyond my mundane parable. You introduced the very thing I wanted to show you without my suggesting it. You introduced Homer into the scenario and showed his impact on the sailors, on the crowd, on the officers of the submarine. The impact of the *Iliad*."

"How do you know what I saw?"

"You were giving a running commentary; giving it so beautifully that I saw through your eyes." She reached out and stroked his hair.

"Peter, you can see visions and give them life. A local habitation and a name. You can be inspired."

He shook his head to clear away the remnants of his dream. "But we didn't react to the Auld like those people down there did to the sub. We attacked—"

"It wasn't the reaction of the Greek sailors. It was the reaction of the sub's captain. You told me how he had the engines stopped, how intently he listened when Homer started to sing."

"Yes." Peter brought the scene back to consciousness. "That skipper listened as though he understood." He chewed his lip, trying to unravel his own riddle. "That sub's forty years obsolete. British schoolboys went on learning Homer long after Greek had been dropped by most schools in the States. Perhaps her skipper—" He laughed. "This is absurd!"

"You made her British in the hope that her skipper remembered enough of his schoolboy Greek to recognize the *Iliad*. And apparently you were right. He did!"

"What does that demonstrate? I mean an hallucination—"

"It demonstrates that a blind singer, in a small Greek town nearly three thousand years ago, was creating something that has outlasted navies and nations. Something that spread out from rugged Chios across the Greek world, across the Roman world, across the whole world. It has spread through the millennia. It will go on spreading, out through the Arm!"

"Out through the Arm? Come off it, Thalia! There aren't even many humans who read Homer anymore."

"Not in the original. But what he said is part of Western civilization. Eastern too, for that matter. More important, he has had excellent translators. Homer in English verse gives much the same pleasure as in archaic Greek. I know. I've read him in both."

"Verse translations of Homer? Whose?"

"Chapman's and Pope's for example."

"That rhymed garbage? Nobody takes them seriously anymore."

"Keats took Chapman very seriously. Shall I quote?"

"No! Please!" He hesitated. "I know those translations were popular enough in their day. But tastes in poetry change."

"Tastes may change. Synapses don't."

"Synapses?"

"Synapses! The junctions between nerve cells in the brain. The one way gates that open and close when you think! Do you think, Peter? Or is your brain just awash with ideas? Didn't you ever learn any science? Any biology?"

"Couldn't see much point. Not when the

damned aliens know it all! Better to learn Greek poetry than the equivalent of Greek science."

"In some ways Greek science had more insight than the aliens have now. Anyway, the synapses are binary units. And binary units are the basis of every intellect in the Arm—living or machine. What has that got to do with outdated translations of Homer? How the hell do you think he could remember the sixteen thousand stanzas of the *Iliad*? He couldn't read because he was blind. He really was. He probably couldn't write. Mycenaean written culture had collapsed." Thalia sat back on her heels. "Peter, I challenge you to recite sixteen consecutive lines of free verse from any modern poet! Any sixteen lines." She folded her arms and waited, unsmiling. His grade twelve English teacher reincarnate.

"I can't remember my own name while you're looking at me like that!" He rubbed his head. "I know modern poetry isn't easily remembered. It's not written to be. We have books now."

"So did Sappho. And I'll bet you can remember everything of hers that survived!"

"Yes—I guess I can. Her sapphics—"

"That's it, Peter! Don't you see? The very essence of poetry, the reason it makes your heart pound, your guts cramp, the hair stand up on your neck is because the rhythm—rhyme, alliteration, stresses, syllable length—any pattern that's a key, that fits the time constants of the synaptic networks. Poetry starts the brain oscillating. Prose can't do that. And for strictly physiological reasons. Brains—all brains—have to be designed so that some subsystems can reverberate. And real poetry can set those systems oscillating!"

Thalia—of course—the Muse of Comedy! She must be joking. He laughed. "So the Muses play on our tuned synapses! Like a harp?"

"Muses! Shit!" She checked as though she had shocked herself as much as she had surprised Peter. "The point I'm trying to drive into your romantic mind is that all brains respond to the beat of stress and rhythm. That's the coded key that opens the synaptic gates! That lets the words get to where they can act. Fire up the emotional brain. Evoke visions! Rouse passions! Why the hell do you think men once believed that poets were magicians?"

"They sure don't believe that now!"

"Because using such crude things as coded keys is beneath the dignity of overintellectual poets. If you don't open the door you can't get in. However wonderful or inspiring your visions— you're shut out!" She paused. "Not just on Earth. That's true about every high-culture race in the Arm."

"You're serious?"

"Damned right I am!" She paused again. "The Auld aren't like that."

"Aren't like what?"

"High-cultured. The others in the Arm sneer at the Auld as ingenuous illiterates—because they don't appreciate high-culture art!" She laughed. "Yet the Auld idea of a wild party is to sit around in groups reciting verse to each other. Trouble is, they haven't got all that of their own, and the high-culture stuff isn't recitable."

"Auld sitting around reciting verse! Like savages round a campfire!" The image was hilarious. "Verbally feeling each other up?"

"A male poet can be as disgusting as any other man! I've always known that!" Her eyes blazed.

He flinched. "Sorry! I thought as Thalia—"

"My namesake's a cruel bitch!" Thalia took a deep breath. "The Auld are sensitive to regular rhythms. They march to a measured tread. The paean suits them fine! Not having much verse of their own, they're getting a taste for ours. Homer's made quite a hit with the Auld."

Homer making a hit with the Auld? How could he?' He looked at her. "I can't swallow that!"

"There's a Cultural Attaché at the Auld Embassy. In fact, there's a dozen of them. Write and ask if they want to see some good verse.

You'll be surprised at the response, though you may not approve of their tastes."

"But why—why haven't I heard about all this?"

"The Auld are as arrogant as Achilles. They hate being laughed at—or patronized. The high-culture races across the Arm have learned not to laugh—but they like to patronize! When the Auld first arrived on Earth they made some tentative approaches. About our arts—especially poetry. The literary experts they consulted—they have great faith in experts—showed what they thought of the Auld taste in verse. They're as sensitive to ridicule as Homer's heroes. But they've got the sensitivity to see that Homer understood and pitied his heroes—arrogance, puerile behavior, cruelty, and everything else. So now the Auld parties go wild over Homer, courtesy of Chapman and Pope. Also other assorted poets—especially the Victorians! Everything with a good meter that makes good sense. The Auld are realists. They don't mind deep meanings so long as there's an understandable surface meaning as well." She looked at Peter in affectionate exasperation. "Shakespeare of course. But Kipling, Keats, Pope, Byron, Tennyson. They're all doing pretty well."

"They're stuck at formalism!"

"If poetry isn't formal it isn't poetry. Chess

without rules isn't chess!" She began to laugh. "We've spent the afternoon talking about words. Peter—only a poet would do that!"

There was the needle! He flushed. Poets talk. Men act. He stood up. "It's getting chilly." The shadow of the mountain had moved over them while they had been talking. "We'd better start for the village."

She came to her feet with an easy grace and slipped her arm in his. "Peter—I haven't enjoyed a day so much in years." And before they had gone halfway down the path they were again sharing a camaraderie he had never before shared with a woman.

Presently he asked, "Is English the only language the Auld have bothered to learn?"

"Yes. They're pragmatists. If one language is enough to communicate with humans, why learn more? But they're a group-think people and when they learn anything they learn it well. All the Transit Authority staff who rotate through the Terran Terminals learn English. So do their diplomats and traders. In fact every Auld who comes to Earth is supposed to speak good English."

"Has to! They won't let us learn Auld."

"They don't let any other race learn Auld. One reason they're language-poor. As poets I mean. They can recite verse beautifully. But they haven't got much of their own to recite.

Bit like the Welsh. Beautiful singers—but I've heard they only have about five songs of their own!"

"The Celts aren't my field." The academic in Peter emerged.

She glanced up at him, frowned, then said, "It's just luck they chose English. Because a Californian team were the first to rupture a Transit. If they'd been Russians, or Germans, or French, or Japanese—then the Auld would be speaking only Russian, or German, or French, or Japanese. And they'd be enjoying Pushkin or Goethe or Verlaine or Hoshi."

"Then they're damned lucky!" said Peter, half-sarcastic, half-serious.

"They really are. Pope's started Ulysses off on an odyssey across the Arm." She looked up into his face. "How about your Aeolic poets— your Alcaeus and Sappho—are their songs going to spread out from Earth? Have their translators done them credit? Will the Auld ever get around to reading those translations?"

"I—I don't know. One of Shelley's is pretty good. Otherwise—there's not much else that would suit their taste. Not as you describe it." He stopped and stared at her, suddenly realizing the import of her claiming to know so much about literature out in the Arm. "Where did you learn all this about the Auld?"

"That, Peter, is none of your business." She

caught his hand. "I don't want to be called 'alien-lover.' Because I'm not! Maybe I'll tell you one day. But not now."

He nodded, disarmed by her touch and her tone, and they walked the rest of the way in friendly silence, parting to go to their rooms with an agreement to meet for dinner.

III

A diplomat, by one definition, is a man who lies for his country, and by any definition his life-style is seen as an index of his country's prestige. The United Nations was as sensitive to prestige as any of its member-states. With Doctor Bose's appointment as a Deputy Director-General had come a number of diplomatic benefits, among them a penthouse apartment in Trygve Lie Towers.

The Doctor was a childless widower who seldom entertained more than one lady at a time, so the apartment was larger than his needs. It included a guest suite usually occupied by some penurious UN delegate to whom he was giving temporary refuge, but it was empty at the time of Sludic's arrival. After a detailed inspection of the suite the Marshal pronounced it as suitable accommodation for himself.

He spent the first few days in it, studying human behavior by watching television despite Bose's repeated statements that what appeared on TV was not typically human. He emerged every evening to join the Doctor at dinner and seemed to enjoy human food while he practiced human table manners. At dinner on the third evening Bose felt they were sufficiently intimate so that he could raise the problem which had brought Sludic to Earth and was disrupting his own life.

"This Alia you're after, did it reach Earth by transit?"

"Yes. There is no other way of crossing space in a reasonable time."

"So it got through your checks on transit passengers?"

"It must have done so. Otherwise it would have been identified at the Terminal. I recently discovered that Alia arrived here several years ago."

"So long?" That meant an alien mimicking a woman had been running loose and unrecognized for years. And it had evaded the Authority's control over access to the Transits; the Transits available to aliens but denied to humans. "If people learn that something looking like a woman has broken through your blockade they'll assume your controls are fallible. That might encourage Terronationalists to take impetuous action." Whenever a Transit Terminal was attacked the Transit Guards reacted by hitting the attackers hard and accurately, but innocent bystanders were always caught in the crossfire. Those were the kind of tragedies it was his job to prevent.

"Good reason to keep secret Alia's presence on Earth. Unless you think you are ready to conduct a successful revolt. In which case the story of Alia's evasion would be valuable propaganda."

Bose knew Sludic was employing neither sarcasm nor humor, but only stating one human alternative. Earth's growing dependence on the Transits made that alternative impractical and gave a bitter undertone to his reply. "How can we hope to displace you now? We can't generate all the electricity we think we require. We can't feed ourselves properly without food from Nuerth. We can't stay prosperous without Arm trade. Most people no longer really want to revolt—whatever they say. But there are fanatics who, if they learn a visitor slipped through your checks, might try to force their way into a Terminal and get killed."

"We no longer have need to kill. Only to stun."

Bose was essentially a pacifist, but the unintended arrogance of the answer would have stung the Mahatma himself. "I suspect there are still some nuclear warheads hidden somewhere." An empty challenge, the riposte of impotent anger.

"There are still many nuclear weapons hidden on Earth. If used they will certainly kill many humans. Some because their fusing and other mechanisms have deteriorated so they are liable to explode on priming. Others, if fired, will activate the shields with even more devastating effects on their users."

Bose shuddered. Twenty years before, after tanks, aircraft, artillery, and infantry had failed to eject the Auld the final attempt had been nuclear. A few Auld and many men and women had been killed or condemned to die slowly before the military had realized that a backwash was set up by an antinuclear shield. He had served with the medical teams struggling to salvage the survivors. "That must never happen again."

"We will best prevent it by ensuring secrecy during our search for Alia, and at its arrest."

"This Alia—is it dangerous in itself?"

"Only when cornered. Then it can be very dangerous." Sludic got up from the table.

"Come, let me show you a schematic of the Spiral Arm. That will help me to fill you in on Alia's background."

Bose followed Sludic into the suite, wondering what he would find. The Marshal had refused maid service and the Doctor expected to see some exotic changes, but none were apparent. The three rooms were spotless, and the alien showed him through them with an element of pride. He was evidently an obsessive-compulsive and a fastidious neatnik. His new suits were hanging neatly in the closet; shaving gear, toothbrushes, towels, antiperspirants, all the paraphernalia of an American male's toilet were in the bathroom, tidily arranged but obviously used. "I have sampled the products advertized on television," Sludic explained. "Some fulfill their claims; others do not." It sounded like his opinion of human society as a whole. He offset this hint of criticism when he escorted Bose back to the lounge. "I enjoyed the books you placed here for my entertainment."

"That wasn't me. UN housekeeping supplies the reading material." Bose glanced at the shelves. It was a standard collection—from the Great Books of the World to pornography aping literature. What was Sludic's reaction to human pornography? All anyone knew about Auld reproduction was that the aliens were hermaphrodites who deposited male and female gametes at designated booths when they wanted to unload. Minute replicas of adult Auld emerged from the resulting conglomerate at a stage of development when they were able to walk but had to be fed. These newborn were adopted by some Auld group and included in the strong network of affection that existed within all pairs, trios, or quartets of adult Auld.

Reproduction was apparently divorced from what humans called "love" and which the Auld, when explaining the basics of their society, called "friendship." All this was quite beyond the man in the street, who wanted to believe the worst of the intruders and called them a bunch of queers who bred in public latrines. Their progeny crawled out of the crap.

"You were going to show me a schematic of the Arm," Bose reminded the Marshal.

"You will see better if I first make it dark." Sludic flicked off the lights, then snapped another switch. A myriad brilliant specks appeared, floating in the middle of the room. "There is the generally accepted schematic of the whole galaxy."

Bose stared. He had pictured the Galaxy as a disc with Earth about two thirds of the way out from the axis. Some thirty thousand parsecs, over a hundred thousand light-years, in diameter; numbers which had no reality. But this glittering model, though only about five meters across, showed the Galaxy's true immensity. He felt insignificant and a little dizzy. The Universe was even stranger than its description in his maternal grandmother's religion.

"The Transit Authority extends over only sixty parsecs of the Spiral Arm." Sludic spoke condescendingly, an Auld attitude which turned even well-disposed humans into resentful critics. "So it is absurd to call us 'Galactics.' There are about one hundred and forty billion stars in the Galaxy, while there are only some seventy thousand in our area of influence. There may be other races with their areas of influence."

"Have you contacted any?"

"Not any civilized races. There are barbarian worlds on the fringes of our system. Earth, for example, was one." Sludic touched a switch and the model exploded, the bright specks racing outward through the walls until there was only a brilliant group hanging in the center of the room. "We connect about three thousand habitable planets." A red spot traced a ruby arc. "There is the frontier of civilization." It jumped beyond the arc to an isolated faintly-glowing speck. "That is Earth."

Beyond the pale, thought Bose. We are only a dim speck beyond the pale.

"The fugitive was first encountered here."

The red spot flicked to the opposite fringe of the group. "We traced it to here—to here—then here—and here." The spot zigzagged across the Arm, leaping from world to world. "This is Larga. Do you know of Larga?"

"No," said Bose. Nor, as far as he knew, did any other human.

"Larga is a data-storage center. Every intelligent race in our system is represented on Larga. They collect, catalog, and store information. They perform a useful service for all civilization."

"Will we have access to Larga?"

"In due course that is possible," said Sludic. An Auld statement which humans had heard so often that it now aroused instant anger. "The fugitive remained on Larga for some time before it revealed its presence. When I went to arrest it, it had already moved. We traced it to here—here—here! Do you see the pattern of its movements?"

"Toward Earth?"

"I doubt it was planning to travel to Earth. My teams were herding it out toward the rim. But as it moved, its alternative directions of flight became increasingly restricted. Finally it arrived on Gadan. Do you know of Gadan?"

"That's the junction where the Californians went before they were shipped on to Nuerth, isn't it?" Doctor Bose felt a dull rage starting to glow within him. "But if this Alia looks human surely it's logical to assume it was heading toward Earth to hide among creatures that looked like itself?"

"I did consider that possibility," agreed Sludic. He did not say why he had rejected it but continued, "Gadan is a minor interchange with only six channels out. By the time the fugitive arrived on Gadan the transit to Earth had been established. That was the one it took."

"You mean that you've hunted this Alia across the Arm and it's been able to dodge you all the way?"

"It has. But no longer. Earth is a dead end. From Alia's previous patterns of escape I have reason to believe that it needs several transits in order to evade our checks. With only two available it is trapped on Earth. All that remains is to run it down. It is for that purpose I have called upon the United Nations for aid."

"How has it managed to fool your teams?"

"In the same manner that it has evaded our teams for so long."

"And how was that?"

"If I knew," snapped Sludic, showing the Auld hypersensitivity to ridicule, "Alia would now be a captive, not a fugitive!"

Bose stared at the cloud of microlights and tried to visualize the maze of Transits between them. He could not picture the complexity of such a three-dimensional weave but he appreciated as never before the immense problems of operating such a system.

He did not understand how the Transits worked; neither did human scientists. The explanation given to children, and which satisfied Bose, likened them to small holes punched through a vast sheet of paper so that to get from one side of the sheet to the other one did not have to travel all the way out to the edge and then all the way back to the center, but could pass almost instantly through the hole.

The Auld knew how to punch such holes in the fabric of subspace. For eons they had been punching holes between worlds, building up a matrix of Transits joining the worlds they judged as civilized. Building, operating, and defending Transits seemed to have become their only racial objective, the main purpose in the life of the individual Auld. Most humans regarded the Auld as an antlike race who excelled only in tunnel-building, a kind of large termite. Bose knew they were far more than that, but what they were he did not know.

The model disappeared and the room lights came on. Bose found Sludic was looking at him with an expression that suggested interest.

"You have never seen this schematic of the Galaxy before?"

"No. I don't think any human has."

"Would you advise us to publish it?"

Bose hesitated. One of the reasons why humans resented the Auld so bitterly was their refusal to share their scientific and technical knowledge. They allowed the import of novel devices from other worlds and did not prevent humans from examining the non-military equipment their teams used outside Terminal territory. They had even allowed humans to keep a flier captured during the confusion of their initial arrival, but twenty years later, human engineers still had no idea why it flew. The Auld acted as if it were enough to demonstrate that some impossibility was possible. If humans could not deduce the mechanism from the embodiment, they were not yet ready to use it.

The general human reaction, after the initial bitter resentment, was the comforting belief that the Auld did not understand how their machines worked, any more than a child who switches on a television set understands electromagnetic theory. Engineers and scientists knew that could not be true, but told each other that, while the Auld might know the workings of their equipment, their technology was now static. Items such as their fliers were unchanged from the fliers they had used millennia before. A few engineers pointed out the fallacy of arguing from the particular to the general; that the fliers were the same because the optimum design had been achieved. That introducing changes for the sake of change was more suggestive of a degenerating technology than of a developing one. But most of humanity had persuaded itself that some race of engineering genius elsewhere in the galaxy was the real developer and producer of the Auld machines. Humans are expert at rationalizing without being rational.

Bose did not believe any of these ego-supporting explanations. He had seen how rapidly the aliens had produced the kinds of food and medications needed by humans to cope with the famines and epidemics raging on after their arrival. This, in fact, had made him resent Auld secrecy the more, because it had proved that their biological sciences were as advanced as their physical. They must have a vast amount of medical knowledge which, if released, could save many human lives and prevent much human suffering.

The refusal of the Auld to tell as well as to show was interpreted by some as part of a plan to keep Earth in subjection. During the first decade after their arrival most research and development had either come to a halt while scientists and engineers waited to hear from their Arm equivalents, or had been diverted into attempts to discover how Auld equipment worked. That initial decade of sterility had changed into a period of renewed R and D as engineers realized there were not going to be any technological handouts. Their self-confidence had recovered with the discovery that there were markets in the Arm for certain sophisticated Terran products. In fact the demand for ultramicrocircuitry, the two megabit chips which had been developed just prior to the Auld arrival, far exceeded Earth's production capacity and was the main reason for its healthy balance of trade. As a result, morale, research, and capital investment had again started to climb and Bose, among others, had begun to appreciate that free information would have stifled human creativity. He was not yet ready to admit that the Auld might have foreseen this and had been protecting humanity from the sterilizing effects of revealed knowledge. But he was thankful for the effect, whatever the cause.

So he did not seize on Sludic's offer to publish the model of the Galaxy as he would have done a few years before. Instead he considered what the effects might be. He knew little about the state of Terran cosmology, except that it had become an historical rather than an exploratory science. The model of the galaxy which Sludic was offering would probably deter any human attempt to explain galactic mechanisms in terms other than those of the alien model. And as it was not the kind of knowledge that would help mankind to solve its immediate problems, Bose's humanitarian drives were not inspired by Sludic's offer. "No. I think it would be intellectually damaging to us if you published it."

Sludic nodded. "I tend to agree with you."

"Most people wouldn't! So please don't tell anybody else that you've told me. Or I'll be even less popular than I am."

"I understand. I'm sorry that your sensitivity to our customs makes you suspect among your own people. There are times when I too sense criticism from my colleagues. If I can do anything to lessen that load, then I will."

"Thanks, Sludic." Bose was surprised and touched by the Marshal's gesture. He knew from his first meeting with the Auld that they would rather help than hinder, so long as the interests of the Transit Authority were not threatened. But he was beginning to detect in Sludic's words and actions something that he would have called common humanity in another human. Perhaps there was indeed an underlying sense of community which permeated all civilized and intelligent beings.

Or perhaps that was wistful thinking and Sludic was only mimicking human sympathy. His success in adopting the physical and behavioral characteristics of a human was astounding. And the fact that he could mimic a man so well made Bose wonder whether Alia, this alien who was passing itself off as a woman, might not also be an Auld.

He glanced at Sludic's face and saw enough grimness behind the calm expression to warn him it would be wiser not to suggest that Alia was a renegade. But that thought led to others. "Many of Alia's movements seem pointless."

"Many of Alia's escapades seem pointless. They are designed to annoy and confuse. So that is their point. Alia is the most mischievously inclined creature I have ever encountered."

"Do you really think that Alia is taking such risks only for the pleasure of annoying you?"

"What other motives could it have? Perhaps to draw attention to itself?" Sludic shrugged.

"Or to draw attention to something else?"

Sludic looked at him sharply. "What do you mean?"

"I may be in danger of offending you, Sludic."

"I will not take offence where none is intended."

"Well—I was thinking—perhaps Alia is trying to draw attention to the weak points in Transit security." When Sludic stared at him in silence, Bose continued, "I mean—the integrity of the transit system is of vital importance to all the worlds it connects. That now includes Earth and Nuerth. So any weaknesses in Transit security are a danger to all of us.'

Sludic frowned and Bose knew he had raised an idea that the Marshal had never considered. There was now probably more emotion than logic in his attitude toward this annoying fugitive. After a moment he said, "That would be an explanation if the Transit Authority reacted angrily to criticisms of its operations. In fact, we welcome them. And we receive many such criticisms. If Alia wishes to bring areas of vulnerability to our attention it can do so easily by pointing them out to us. Anonymously if it did not wish to be identified, although it would forgo the usual reward a justified complainant receives."

"I see. Yes—I suppose that can't be Alia's motivation." Bose returned to his study of Alia's antics. He still felt the motive behind them must be more cogent than mischief. Such as holding the Transit Authority up to ridicule?

IV

Peter Ward stood looking from his window at the moon-washed Aegean and cursed his cowardice. He had spent the best evening of his life with a woman he already loved. She had listened to his theory on the orientation of Doric temples and, better still, had understood it. She had persuaded him to recite more of his poetry; her appreciation had seemed genuine and her comments had been appropriate. She had been sympathetic when he had described the dilemmas which a young scholar had to face. She had told him little about herself but she had let him know that she was twenty-eight, single, and without emotional attachments. Her intelligence was as obvious as her beauty. She was educated and wealthy, but she had not dropped even a hint about the source of her education or her wealth. Her sudden flashes of blazing anger were frightening, but quickly turned into warm affection. When she had left him to go to bed she had kissed him lightly on the lips.

He had stood like a star-struck idiot, watching her disappearing into her room, letting her get away without even an attempt to hold her. The kiss had left him incapable of speech or movement. Now, in his own room, he could only clench his fists and curse his stunned response.

Ten minutes later, while he was still gathering sufficient courage to go and tap on her door, she tapped on his. "I think it's better if we use your room," she explained as he let her in, and before he could answer her arms were around him.

His body had responded before his mind could consider. Once committed, Peter was a sensitive lover and within seconds he realized that he was exploring a passionate ignoramus whose knowledge of sex was theoretical. But an ignoramus eager to learn and delighted in learning. Maneuvers which had been routine with his previous partners she greeted as exciting novelties. To the joy of becoming her lover was added the pleasure of being her teacher.

A role he had never played before, nor expected to play with any woman. When, swept onward by their common passion, she gave a little gasp of pain and a momentary resistance he thought it was his clumsiness and became even more gentle. But she urged him on with such fervor that it was only after they had, at last, fallen apart that he panted he was sorry, that he hadn't dreamed she was a virgin.

"But I'm not! Not anymore!" She laughed and kissed him. "Tell the maid that you cut yourself shaving in bed."

He laughed with her, took her back into his arms, and eventually they fell asleep together.

He woke to find her standing naked by the window, gazing toward the rising sun. He waited sleepily for her to start singing, and when she remained silent he mumbled from beneath the pillow, "Why don't you sing that song again?"

"What song?"

"The song you sang yesterday morning. Up at the temple."

She was beside the bed in an instant, gripping his shoulder. "Peter, what did you hear me sing?"

He came awake. "That song by Sappho, her Hymn to Aphrodite. At least the first five stanzas are by Sappho. I'd never heard the rest before. Who wrote them? They're damned good. Where can I find a copy?"

Her nails dug into his bare shoulders. "Peter—wake up and listen to me!"

"I am awake!" He sat up and kissed her to prove it.

She stood before him, naked and intense. "Peter—you must promise me never, not under any circumstances, to mention that song to anyone. Nor that you heard me sing it."

"Why not? It's good enough to be genuine Sappho."

"It may have been by Sappho. No, don't ask me more! Just promise that you'll forget it."

She was radiating such wrath that he did not argue. She must have a manuscript with the whole poem, and was preparing it for publication. He could understand her alarm. Fragments of Sappho were still turning up on Egyptian papyri, and a complete poem would be a major literary coup, even in the present unliterary times.

"Promise me!" she urged, leaning over him, her hair glowing in the morning sunlight, her blue eyes blazing.

Her perfume, the nearness of her body, roused his desire and made him stubborn. "Two conditions. I'll promise on two conditions."

"What conditions?"

"One—that you send me the manuscript. So

I can be the first out with a translation when you do publish."

She straightened and swept her hair back over her white shoulders. "All right. I'll send you a copy of the Greek. And you can publish a verse translation if you want to. As long as you don't connect it with Sappho. In fact, as long as you don't say it's a translation from anyone.'

"I wasn't thinking of making a verse translation!"

"You'll translate it into English verse or you won't get it to translate!"

"Okay—okay! Verse it is."

"And your second condition?"

"That you promise to phone me when I'm back at Cornell. So I can see you again."

She sat down slowly on the bed and looked at him with a worried affection. "Peter—that might not be wise. Not for you. Not for me. It would be better to remember only how we made love on this island."

"Is there some other guy?"

She shook her head.

"A girl perhaps?"

She shook it more emphatically.

"Then I must see you again. Promise that I will and I'll promise to keep your secret. At least until after you've published the original."

She sighed, but did not seem unhappy at the

compromise he had forced on her. "I'll contact you within sixty days—if I can. That's the only promise I can make."

"And you'll send me a copy of that song?"

"I'll mail it when I get to Athens."

"Okay—then I'll keep your sapphics a secret."

"Don't ever mention it again."

"I'll never mention it to anyone but you."

She tried to persuade him not to mention it even to her, but he pulled her down onto the bed and swept her away into love and forget-fulness.

With full daylight some of the wariness she had shown the previous day returned. She went from the bed to the window and looked down toward the harbor. "Peter, I think that's the ferry."

"Relax! There's no hurry. His Greasiness told me they'll be working cargo all day. She's not due to sail until late afternoon. We've still got the day to ourselves. Come back to bed."

"Not now." She continued to stare toward the harbor so intently that Peter, grumbling, crawled off the bed and went to stand beside her. The ferry was just coming alongside and he could see nothing unusual about the boat, nor about the people standing on the decks and crowding the wharf.

"What's up?" he asked, infected by her tension.

"Nothing important." She turned from the window and gave him a quick kiss. "I'd better get dressed." Before he could persuade her to exchange lovemaking for dressing she had grabbed her wrapper and was gone from his room.

Disappointed and annoyed he pulled on his own clothes, then stood indecisive. Who was she expecting? A lover or a husband? No, that was impossible—unless the man was impotent. But she had clamped up when she'd seen that ferry. He watched the gangway being run out and the first passengers starting to come ashore. Goaded by love and concern he left his room and strode down the passage, determined to discover what was upsetting her. He burst in on her without thought and without knocking. Then he froze.

She was dressed in her blue jumpsuit and had been standing at the window, looking down the main street toward the harbor. When she heard the door open she had swung round and Peter found himself staring at the muzzle of an automatic.

The blaze in her eyes was replaced by a frown of annoyance as she lowered the weapon. "Peter!"

He did not move and all he could find to say was, "Those things are illegal!"

"But sometimes necessary."

"Why? What?"

"That's none of your business."

"Oh yes it is!" He stepped forward, grabbed her shoulders, and almost shook her. "I love you! That makes your business, my business. What the hell's going on?"

For a moment he thought she was going to knock his hands away, but she only sighed. "I warned you against getting involved with me."

"I thought you were warning me about some trouble you've got back in the States. You didn't say anything about guns here on Psara."

"I didn't think there'd be any trouble here. I'm still not sure there is."

"Whatever's happening, I'm involved already. Involved because I love you."

She eased his hands from her shoulders and beckoned him over to the window. "You see that man standing on the wharf? The one in a dark suit. Big man. Dressed like a German tourist."

"Yes. He's sure no Greek."

She handed him a pair of binoculars. "Take a good look at him. What do you see?"

Peter studied the face floating before him. "Faces aren't trustworthy indicators of character. He's probably a kind-hearted family man from Hamburg. But he looks like a cold-blooded brute!"

"I've seen him once before. He may be a family man from Hamburg but he's not kind-hearted. When I saw him he was kicking information out of a bellhop in Athens."

"Information? Information about what?"

"Information about me!" She took the glasses back and returned to studying the other passengers as they came ashore. "I'm certain he's not alone. I'm trying to identify his fellow thugs. Ah! I think that's one."

"Who? Why?" The big man had turned and was slowly leaving the wharf.

"That squirt in mechanic's coveralls, toting a toolbox. The big guy started to move as soon as he saw him coming down the gangway. Now—if the squirt—yes! He's waiting for somebody else. And there she is. A woman, by God! And a real bitch, by the look of her."

A woman with the build of a wardress and the face of a whore was coming across the deck of the ferry. The mechanic waited, as if making sure that the woman had seen him. Then he too turned and followed the big man up the village street. The woman reached the wharf, picked up a suitcase from the pile of luggage, and followed the mechanic. "Only three of them," said Thalia, lowering her glasses.

"What's this all about?"

"Peter, if you want to help me you've got to trust me. And do exactly as I say. Understand?"

"No, but—"

"Without asking questions!" She had changed from lover to goddess, from pupil to teacher.

He stood in silence beside her as the three from the ferry came up the street, fifty meters apart, three people acting as if they were strangers. The big man sat down at a table outside the cafe across from the hotel, the mechanic went into the cafe's dark interior, the woman came into the hotel.

Thalia drew Peter away from the window. "I have to find out why they're following me, so I must get them alone. The woman's probably checking if I'm staying here. Ah—she's found I am." The woman had emerged from the hotel, taken a table on the veranda below, and was ordering breakfast.

Thalia put her automatic in her valise, tapped the pouch belted to her waist, and went to the door. 'I'm going to walk up the path to the temple. As soon as I'm out of sight one of those three may follow. They'll probably use the same pattern as they did coming ashore—at least they will if they're as good at their job as I think they are. Watch for the second to leave, then the third. Tell me the order when I get back."

"But what do I *do*?"

"I've just told you. Stay here and watch the order they take when they leave."

"You expect me to stay here while those three thugs trail you to a deserted temple? What do you think I am? I'm going across the road to ask that big klutz what the hell he wants. And then tell him to lay off you!"

She gave a slight smile and laid her hand on his arm. "When you're dealing with buzzards you have to do it their way! All right, Peter, if you want a part of the action, this is what you'll do. Follow the third, stay out of sight, and don't join in unless you see I'm in real trouble. How's that?"

"I'd rather be with you."

"If you're with me that shark won't bite. He'll wait for a time and place which will be better for him and worse for me. Here and now is my chance to find out what they're after. Will you do as I ask?"

Peter nodded reluctantly.

"Do you want a gun? I'm leaving mine here in the valise."

He shook his head.

She shrugged. "It's your decision." She opened the door. "Follow whoever's last. And stay out of sight. Now—I'm off. That bitch has ordered breakfast. If I'm right she won't stay to eat it. She'll start out mad and hungry!" Then she was gone along the passage and down the stairs to the lobby. Peter returned to the window feeling that a true hero would have been doing something else.

The woman had bitten into a roll and was about to pour herself coffee when Thalia walked across the veranda and turned to stroll up the street. The woman jumped to her feet, cursing as she spilled her coffee. Thalia reached an alley between two houses and disappeared round the corner. The woman started after her. A moment later the waiter came onto the veranda to shout about the bill and curse all tourists.

As the woman turned into the alley the mechanic emerged from the darkness of the cafe, toolbox in hand, and went after her. Moments later the big man paid his bill, rose from his table, and trudged after the mechanic. Peter went racing down the stairs, and reached the street just as the big man disappeared between the houses.

For the first time in his life Peter was glad of his grounding in urban guerrilla tactics. Methods of following alien-lovers marked for assassination had been drummed into him, and his training made him feel more confident as he shadowed the big man out of the village and up the path toward the temple of Aphrodite.

It wound and dipped its way over the coarse grass and outcroppings of rock, becoming fainter and fainter as tourists, its only users, had turned back from the climb. The big man quickened his pace, presumably in response to the mechanic ahead, and Peter was beginning to breathe heavily when he rounded a turn behind the ridge above the temple and found the man standing some thirty meters away, gazing out to sea. He was evidently acting as a rearguard but had not expected to find anyone behind him, for his expression on seeing Peter was a startled scowl.

Peter continued to advance as if he were indeed a tourist enjoying the view. The big man ignored him until they were almost abreast of each other, and then swerved in a planned stumble, at the same time growling, "Bloody Englishman! Think you own the road?"

Had Peter been the usual inoffensive tourist he would have been knocked sideways by the man's shoulder and then have retreated from a bully trying to pick a fight. And that, of course, was the object of the maneuver. But Peter was not the usual tourist and recognized a standard tactic the moment before the other lunged. He swayed sideways so the man tripped over his outstretched foot, went sprawling, and confirmed his Germanic origin by his oaths.

Peter's self-confidence soared with success. He stood apologizing imitating the confused tourist who didn't know what was happening.

He even produced a fake English accent. "I'm frightfully sorry! I didn't mean to get in your way. And you've skinned your hands, by George!"

The German growled and charged, launching a blow calculated to floor the intruder without doing major damage. Peter, with no reason to pull his own punch, dodged the blow, sank his fist into the other's stomach and, as he doubled up, drove a knee into his face.

The man went to the ground, pulling a gun from a shoulder-holster. Peter kicked him, hissed, "I'm no bloody Englishman!" grabbed the gun, and stood back.

A scream came from beyond the ridge. The German groaned and sat up. Peter knocked him cold with the butt of the pistol and raced up to the crest.

The woman had Thalia backed against one of the temple pillars and had started to work her over. The mechanic was reading questions from a sheet of paper, and the woman was slapping Thalia's face after each question. She screamed again as Peter reached the ridge and it almost brought him sliding down the scree in a charge to her rescue.

His common sense saved him from suicide. A frontal attack would only get him shot. He went scrambling along the ridge just behind the crest, planning to fire at Thalia's tormentors from close range. Even if he didn't hit them he would drive them to cover and give her a chance to run; he had seen how fast she could run.

There was an agonized howl from the vicinity of the temple and it swamped his common sense. He slid down the ridge and charged berserk across the plateau, gun in hand. He pulled himself up abruptly when, for the second time that morning, he found himself facing the muzzle of Thalia's automatic. She was standing over the woman who, like the mechanic, was writhing on the ground, and her welcome was not warm.

"Oh—it's you! Where's the big thug?"

"Knocked out! Back on the path," panted Peter. "I've got his gun."

"Good." She said it without enthusiasm. "Go over there and watch out in case he wakes up." She began to study the paper the mechanic had been holding.

Peter went to the edge of the promontory, disappointed and confused. Presently Thalia looked from the paper to the mechanic. "Quite a questionnaire, eh? Things your boss wants to know scattered among questions to which he'd given you the answers. So when I started to sing you could check I was singing the right tune and give me the treatment if I was off key!" She kicked over the mechanic's toolbox.

Then she kicked the mechanic. "You little worm! You've even brought a battery-operated shocker!"

The man tried to roll away from her, his muscles knotted into cramps, and he lay still. "We was just trying to get the answers to some questions," he whined.

"Who paid you to ask 'em?" Thalia knelt beside him.

"Look Miss, if I tell you, 'e'll kill me!"

"Do you want me to do a test run on you with your own gear?"

The man shuddered, but stayed silent.

Thalia stood up. "Peter—come over here!"

Peter came reluctantly. "Darling, don't you think—?"

"No, I don't! Take their guns."

Relieved that she hadn't told him to do anything more brutal, he searched the shivering Cockney, found a revolver, and put it carefully down on the grass. Then he approached the woman, uncertain of where to look.

"Between her legs! Under her skirt! Oh—for God's sake!" as Peter continued to hesitate. "There!" She jerked up the woman's dress exposing two broad bare thighs with a holstered automatic on the right. "Grab that. Then throw it—and his—over the cliff."

Peter, avoiding the woman's venemous glare, took the automatic from the holster, collected the Cockney's revolver, and sent both guns spinning toward the sea far below. Then he stood waiting, hoping she wasn't going to involve him further in whatever she was about to do.

She didn't have to do much. Something had shaken loose inside the Cockney for when she went toward him he squealed, "Lay off me, Miss! I'll talk! Only for Gawd's sake don't tell nobody I did." He rolled an eye toward the woman. "If you split on me, you bitch, I'll kill you for sure."

"It's Pirenne," spat the woman. Her accent was pure Chicago.

"Pirenne?" Thalia turned. "That information broker? The one who works out of Paris?"

"I don't know where he hangs out. No— honest I don't!" She shrank back. "I'm telling the truth. I know you can make us squeal. Anybody can make anybody squeal if they've the guts to lean hard. And you have! Start on Harry! He'll sing at the first shock!"

"It's Pirenne, Miss," whined Harry. "Like she says."

"Who's the boss of this operation? The big kraut back up the trail?"

"You mean 'Erman? 'E don't know nuffink. He's all shit and muscle. We 'ired 'im for his strength."

"Then who's the boss around here?"

"She is!"

"Are you?" Thalia looked at the woman. She gave a sullen nod.

"What's your name?"

"Rosie."

"Rosie what?"

"Rosie Shaw. And that's the truth. I swear!"

Thalia took several brisk turns up and down the promontory, then returned to stand over her. Rosie's cramps had disappeared but she still seemed too weak to move. When she tried to roll away, Thalia caught her shoulder and pushed her onto her back. "Don't try it! You won't be able to walk for another ten minutes. And I can twist you both up again any time I want to."

"We won't try nothin', Miss!" said Harry.

"Okay! Do you want to make a deal?"

"You bet, Miss!"

"Depends what the deal is," said Rosie. "No good making a deal if you can't deliver."

"If I tell you what Pirenne wants to know. If I give you the answers to these questions." She held up the questionnaire. "Answers that'll make Pirenne happy, will you answer my questions?"

"Sure we will, Miss."

"Trouble is—we don't know much," said Rosie, licking her lips and fumbling weakly with her skirt.

"You may know something useful. And I can tell when you're lying without any trick questions!" Thalia glanced from the man to the woman and Peter saw them flinch. "The first lie I hear—from either of you—and I'll have both of you turning yourselves into pretzels! Understand?"

"We sure do," said Rosie, the sweat coming out on her forehead.

"You get paid when you take this back to Pirenne completed. Right, Rosie?"

"We mail it. Pirenne never sees the people he hires."

"You mail it with the answers. If he likes 'em you pick your dough up at a drop-off? Right?"

"Right, Miss."

"And he's not interested in how you got the answers, eh?"

"That's the way Pirenne operates. That's how he never gets any muck on his hands." Rosie rubbed her wrists.

"Then here's the deal. I give you the answers. Pirenne'll like 'em—I promise you that! Then you collect your fees and fade. So everybody's happy." She looked up, saw Peter listening, and snapped, "Peter—go and make sure Hermann's still out!"

"Darling, don't you think—?" He saw her expression and began to climb up the scree.

When he reached the ridge he stopped to look back down at the tableau on the ruined floor of Aphrodite's temple. Rosie was scribbling down answers which Thalia was dictating. He couldn't hear what she was saying but he suspected it was something illegal. Why was she making a deal with that pair of crooks? How had she sent both of them writhing onto the grass? What the hell was going on? Who the hell was she?

Again he had the uneasy feeling that she was some kind of a goddess. She had the essential characteristics. Beautiful and passionate, kind and cruel, capricious and determined. A skewed sense of right and wrong. Her love had inspired him. Her anger had scorched him.

But last night she'd been only a woman. And she'd be only a woman again. He'd make sure of that! He looked down once, then turned his back on something he didn't want to watch and started along the path.

Hermann was sitting up. He tried to get to his feet when he saw Peter, then sat down again when he saw the gun. Peter stood beyond his reach and the two stared at each other with mutual loathing.

They stared at each other for some twenty minutes, and then Rosie and Harry appeared, pushing an apparently battered Thalia between them. Peter started up the path, preparing to make another rescue attempt, and then realized she was faking for Hermann's benefit.

"It's no good, mate!" Harry shouted. "We've got what we came after. You can 'ave her back now. She ain't badly damaged."

"You bastards!" spat Peter, as infuriated by Harry's acting as by the sight of Thalia's simulated tears.

Harry ignored him but started to bait Hermann. "Let 'im jump you, did you, Fatso? We orter cut your pay for that! Nearly fouled up everything, 'e did. Coming on us, sudden-like!"

"Stow it, Harry!" snapped Rosie. "Hermann gets paid, like we agreed." She went to examine the gash on the German's forehead. "Pistol-whipped you, did he?" She glared at Peter. "You like hitting people, eh?"

"You lying broad—" Peter spluttered.

Harry pushed Thalia into his arms. "Take her off and clean her up, mate!"

"Please!" She clutched him. "Take me away from this horrible place!"

He put his arm round her shoulders, comforting her automatically while still keeping Hermann covered. "What's the deal?"

"They let us get on the boat this afternoon. They're staying on the island. A plane's coming tomorrow to pick them up." She pressed her tear-stained face against his shoulder. "Please—take me back to the hotel!"

Her acting as so good that for a moment he was convinced she was a hurt human girl. He squeezed her and they started down the path together. Harry shouted after them, "It wasn't 'is fault we jumped you, Miss. You got yourself a good bodyguard. Better than 'Ermann 'ere!"

"About as dumb as Hermann!" Thalia muttered into Peter's shirt, reminding him what she was.

As they picked their way toward the village he remembered that while it is dangerous to wound a goddess it may be even more dangerous to see one in a situation where she does not wish to be seen.

They stood together leaning on the rail of the ferry, watching Psara disappear astern. "Now," said Peter, "tell me what all that was about."

Thalia had spent the day vacillating between icy anger and hot affection. In the hotel she had met his questions with promises that she'd explain when they were aboard the ferry. She was still reluctant. "Peter, the less you know about me the better for you."

"I must know about you!" He took her by the shoulders and, despite the flare of anger in her blue eyes, he turned her to face him. "You're the loveliest woman I've ever seen. You speak Aeolic Greek. You can call up visions and knock crooks into cramps. You're twenty-eight, and you were a virgin! You know more about the Arm than anyone I've heard of. You entrance me—and you scare the hell out of me." He kissed her. "More important—I love you. And you—well, you respond to me." He kissed her again, and for longer.

Her lips were hard—then soft. The tip of her tongue—she broke away. "I can't—I mustn't—!"

"You must!" He hesitated. "At least explain what happened up at the temple. What deal did you make with those crooks? If that guy Pirenne hears about me, he's liable to think I'm your accomplice in crime." Peter grinned at her human scowl. "I'd like to be!"

"Crime? I haven't committed any crime!" She bit her lip. "Okay—I'll tell you the background to that face-off." She put her arms on the rail and stared down at the waves racing past. "I made my money from diamonds. Prospecting for 'em on Nuerth."

"From what?"

"Finding diamonds. You know—the things some women hang from their ears. The hardest and strongest material there is. Hard to find and hard to make—even for the supertechs in the Arm. Sintered diamond is ultrahard. So even if women didn't wear 'em the high-techs need 'em. And pay for 'em. There's a good market for diamonds all over the Arm."

"I'll take your word for it!"

"I found a pipe on Nuerth. A pipe's a place where there are lots of diamonds. A lot more than I needed. I brought enough back to Earth to set me up for life."

"You mean—you dug 'em yourself? Prospecting?" He stared down at her, trying to imagine her trudging through the mountains carrying a pickaxe and leading a mule.

"What the hell's so strange about my prospecting?" Her expression made her look tough enough to prospect for anything. "I tried to keep the news of my strike secret, but those things leak out. A lot of people wanted in."

"Pirenne one of 'em?"

"Indirectly. He's an information broker. Trades information—mostly industrial information obtained illegally. He knows who knows what and who will pay to know it. Traders were ready to pay to find that pipe. But they couldn't find me. Once I'd unloaded the rocks I faded. Too much harassment—offers dangerous to reject! I thought I'd covered my tracks. But Pirenne ran me down last year and made me an offer like that. I refused. Today was his second bid."

"When I left you were telling those crooks something. Where you found your diamonds?"

She looked out to sea and nodded. "I gave them the coordinates."

"Gave? For free?"

"For free. I just wanted to get Pirenne off my back." She turned to face him. "Peter—I've got a cabin."

"A cabin?" Nothing was important except the promise in her eyes. "How? There aren't any."

"The Skipper has a small stateroom. Lets his friends use it. I made friends with him on the trip to Psara. He said I can have it for the crossing. Save me from sleeping on deck. There's only a single bunk, so we'll have to share." She smiled an Aphrodite smile.

"It's getting chilly up here." He was starting to sweat. "Let's go below."

In the small compartment with the steel bulkheads around and the throb of the engines below only the precious present existed. Her body against his, her parted lips, her closed eyes, the flush rising to her cheeks; a very passionate and very human woman. Then her hair brushed his face and he caught her scent. Her aura touched his mind and he pushed her away.

Her eyes opened, damp with desire, then hot with anger. "What's that for?"

He stammered, "I can't—Thalia—I'm afraid!"

Half-naked, her need as evident as his, she sat up on the bunk. "You want some kind of a confession before you'll make love? Erotic blackmail?"

"No! No—I swear! It's just—while I'm not sure what you are—!" He stood up.

"You think I'm a lamia or something?"

"Not a lamia!" Or something? "I'm scared!"

"And you can't make love while you're scared?"

He nodded, miserable.

"If I tell you—that'll break your block?"

"I—I think so."

"A poet's trap!" Her expression mixed doubt with desire. "Like they used to say—love is lunacy. Avoid it! I did—until I met you. Peter— do you love me?"

"I do. Really, I do! It's just—I can't control my imagination."

"Your imagination! Of course! You're a poet! My bad luck—my first love's a poet! Any other kind of man would have taken me—no questions asked." She fought her frustration. "Death to mock a poet! Death to love a poet! Death to be a poet! Very well, Peter, my love, you've asked for it. You'll wish you hadn't!"

Her anger sparked his own. "Why? I don't give a damn what you've done. I just want to know what you are. Why should I be afraid of the truth?"

"Because it's a truth that's dangerous to know."

"If you're not a goddess—quit acting like one! If you're another mortal—treat me like one. Tell me the truth. I can handle it!"

"Then sit down!" She pointed to the bunk and when he subsided onto it she leaned toward him, her glowing hair falling about her white shoulders. "Here's all you need to know. I'm as human as you are. But I have been off-Earth— and not just to Nuerth. I've been through the Transits to other worlds in the system. I've learned about the Auld—and I've learned a lot of other things too. Evoking dreams in a lover and sending enemies spastic are just a couple of 'em."

"You've been—? You know—?" He jumped to his feet. "Then you can fake a Transit entry? You can tell us how to screw those aliens?"

"Screw the Auld?" She laughed. "That's beyond me. Or anybody else!"

"But you've told the government? The UN?"

"Like hell! I've told nobody except you. And I'm beginning to wish I hadn't told you." She paused. "Peter—can't you guess what's likely to happen to me if some group—some government—on Earth learns I know how to get off it? If they think that I have the key to the stars?"

"Happen to you? You'd be a hero! You'd be the goddess who set us free! You'd—!" He stopped as he thought. "They'd use you!"

"And I won't be used. Not the way they'd want."

"They'd make you. Oh God!" He sat down again. His time as a Terran activist had taught him something of the despicable means even decent men and women will use to reach their ideal end.

"Exactly. They wouldn't believe my warnings. If I didn't cooperate in some crazy plan they'd try and grind it out of me. And I'll die before I'll open the door to Hades!" She gripped his arm. "Peter, by telling you even that much I've put my sanity—my life—in your hands. Proof of love? It does make you act mad!"

"I'll never tell anyone. I swear!"

"Then you'd better make sure nobody learns what you know. If they find out—you'll tell! Sooner or later. Information extraction technology has advanced a long way on Earth since the days of the rack. That little worm's box of electronic tricks is primitive compared to what's available."

"What are you going to do?"

"That's more than you need to know. Right now—I intend to make you make love to me!" She pulled him down onto the bunk, on top of her.

And when they lay, satiated and exhausted, she whispered into his ear, "Peter, you'll never forget about us. That I swear. But I'd like you to forget what I told you about me. About where I've been. What I know. Safer for both of us. Can I help you to do some selective forgetting?"

"Perform any magic you like on me! You've bewitched me already. Anything—just so long as you don't forget me."

"I'll never forget you, Peter! My sweet poet!" She began to kiss his eyelids, stroke his body, whisper more words into his ear.

He drifted away into dreams. When he awoke in her arms most of what he remembered seemed only another wonderful dream.

V

Sludic, after two weeks in New York, was still spending his evenings watching television, but now he was doing it in the company of Doctor Bose. He emerged from the seclusion of his suite to sit in the doctor's favorite armchair and ask questions about what was happening on the TV screen. Bose, who detested television, had to watch it with him and began to appreciate the intense loneliness that Sludic was enduring in his unnatural solitude. For an Auld to be parted from his group was painful in itself; to be alone among humans was more than most could have survived.

The Marshal's English was now fluent, but he was still confusing the programs with the advertisements. On his fifteenth evening as a house guest he was asking Bose why the lady in the picture was promoting toilet paper by pressing the stuff against her cheeks, when the telephone rang. Bose used the call to escape, and when he returned he switched off the TV. "That was the Unipol Identification Center. They have sixteen possible matches with Alia's picture. I'm having them sent over now."

Sludic sat up. "Is that safe?"

"As safe as nervous diplomats can make it. The duty officer at the Identification Center didn't know who she was speaking to. The Center never knows who asked for a match but ships the drop to Unipol Exchange. Exchange checks for explosives, puts it through a coded shuffle, and a dispatcher tubes it to me without knowing what's in it or where it's from."

"Ah! Human paranoia!"

"Only paranoid politicians and nervous diplomats survive." Bose was saved from having to expand on his statement by a ping from the pneumatic delivery system as a package arrived. He opened it and handed the sixteen photographs inside to the Marshal, keeping the identification list for himself. "You make the first pass."

Sludic seated himself at the table, arranged the photographs face-down in a neat pile, and began to turn them up one by one, as though playing solitaire. When he turned up the fourth he said, "That resembles Alia."

Bose looked over his shoulder and laughed. "That's a statue, not a person." He checked the identification list. "A statue of Pallas Athene, a Greek goddess, after Praxiteles. Fourth century B.C. Some humorist must have stored the picture and that dumb machine—"

"Nevertheless it resembles Alia. Can you not see the likeness?"

Bose agreed there was a vague resemblance. "Athena represents a type of woman one still sees among the Greeks."

Sludic nodded and continued to turn up photographs. At the tenth he stopped. "That is certainly Alia."

"She's no statue. But she may be Greek. That picture's identified as 'Unknown woman, Athens Airport, 1635 hrs 20th May.'" He studied the photograph. "She does look like your Alia. And she hasn't changed much. This was taken only six weeks ago. When was yours taken?"

Sludic's eloquent silence indicated that he was not going to say when his picture of Alia had been taken.

"She's at the US National Airlines counter, and it's four in the afternoon. So she's probably about to leave for the States. But why should anybody take a picture of an unknown woman and then file it with Unipol?"

"It's the kind of trick Alia herself might play. She is fond of pointless but irritating jests!" Sludic continued to inspect photographs.

Bose wondered whether his use of "she" meant anything. "Do you want me to have the FBI follow up on this picture?"

"Why the FBI?" Sludic had found no other likeness and was comparing the photo of Pallas Athene with that of the woman in the airport.

"If she was flying from Athens to North America, she's probably in the United States now."

"Are not the FBI inclined to precipitate violence?"

"Only in movie reruns. Now-a-days they spend more time examining corporate accounts than interrogating people. Also—I can trust the FBI to start a search for the woman in that photograph without alerting her or anybody else."

"It is vital that Alia be not alerted! I cannot overemphasize her skill in deception and evasion. In her imaginative tactics." He paused, then added, "Those are among the most cogent reasons for my belief that she is not human."

"I appreciate your point!" said Bose, sinking into a chair.

"Pardon. I did not mean to offend." During

the previous week Sludic had seemed to realize that brief barked remarks were considered rude. "I am only pointing out that we are dealing with an exceptionally cunning individual who has evaded me for much longer than I care to contemplate. Whom I have hunted across the Arm. If she gets even a hint that I have traced her to Earth she will start to take precautions which will make it more difficult for even your police forces to run her down."

"I understand," said Bose, wishing Sludic wouldn't overcompensate by piling subclause upon subclause; he found the Marshal's habit catching as well as tiring. "When I brief the agents I'll emphasize that their search and supervision must be discreet. The FBI are expert in discreet surveillance. I speak from personal experience. They had me under surveillance for three years before I even suspected I was being watched."

"They had you under surveillance! Why?"

"Because I seemed to have an unusually good relationship with you aliens. That marked me as a probable traitor."

"Do they still have you under surveillance? Because if they are watching you they will have become aware of me."

"I stopped that nonsense as soon as I became a Deputy DG. I kicked a number of asses— kicked them hard!" He saw the question forming on Sludic's lips. "That's a metaphor—not a form of physical punishment! I mean I made sure I came off their list. I'm part of the power group now. You're still anonymous."

Sludic spent a few moments digesting all this, and then asked, "Is my imitation of a human good enough for me to be present when you meet with those FBI agents?"

Bose studied the Marshal. "You look like a man. When you're dressed nobody'll suspect you're anything else, though you'd better not take off your jacket." Sludic's mimicry had only extended to imitating the general shape and the exposed areas of a human body. When he was under the shower he was certainly not human. "Your accent is now perfect TV. Your vocabulary and syntax are, if anything, too good. You won't betray yourself in how you talk, but you might by what you say. There's still a lot of Auld arrogance in your remarks. So—yes, your imitation's good enough to meet the FBI, as long as you keep your mouth shut."

Sludic nodded. "I will therefore keep my mouth shut unless I have to breathe through it."

Bose glanced at him, then dismissed the thought that the Marshal might be attempting humor. "What I mean is—ask direct questions, but avoid adding your opinions. It's those that sound unhuman."

"Thank you, Alex. You know how much I appreciate your candid advice."

Bose was too surprised at Sludic using his personal name to wonder if the Marshal was now attempting sarcasm.

He showed only detached interest the next day when he sat in Bose's office listening to the Doctor trying to sound like a senior officer of Unipol. Issuing military-type orders was not Bose's usual way of communicating with his staff, and the two agents assigned to the operation had soon realized that their new chief, this short plump Doctor of mixed racial origin, was no security specialist by either aptitude or experience. They listened to him repeating the same instructions in different words with polite condescension.

That attitude was the only superficial characteristic they shared. Gerald Quine was a cold-eyed man of around forty who reminded Bose of the ancient FBI movies he had watched as a boy. Katina Plastiras was a black-haired fresh-faced young woman whose firm figure and ready smile suggested a tourist guide rather than a Federal Officer. Bose had asked that one of the agents be fluent in Greek to follow up the Athens end of the trail, and he assumed she was the only one available.

He had already given each of them a photograph of Alia, impressed on them the sensitivity of the operation, and let them assume that Lester Sloan (as he had introduced Sludic) was a senior official in the current Administration. A successful outcome of the search would therefore aid the Agency to obtain the increase in funds it was seeking from Congress.

"It is of the highest national and international importance that we discover the identity and whereabouts of that woman. The only information we have is her picture and the Athens' airport match made by Unipol's computers. It was taken at sixteen-twenty three weeks ago and from her position in the airport she had probably come from or was en route to the United States."

"We have already gathered that, Doctor." Gerald Quine put the photograph in his pocket; Katina Plastiras put hers in her purse. They both rose to go.

"You understand—she must not be alarmed. She must not be allowed to suspect she is under surveillance."

"You have already emphasized that to us, Doctor." Katina gave a kind smile. The kind given by teachers of backward children.

"Do you have any other instructions?" asked Quine, with the expression of a G-Man about to hunt Public Enemy Number One.

"Yes—no—only to emphasize that this is a

most sensitive operation. For both the United Nations and the United States. Report only to me and in person. Is that clear?"

"You've made it quite clear, Doctor," smiled Katina. "I assume we can phone you?"

"Phone? Yes—call me if you have to. But don't give me any information."

Sludic spoke for the first time. "Doctor Bose is naturally concerned about possible wire-taps. So use discretion in what you say on the telephone."

Both agents looked at him with automatic respect. Here was a man who sounded as if he knew what he was doing, whatever that might be. "We understand, sir," said Quine.

"We'll move off immediately, sir," said Katina.

"Do that," said Sludic with the confidence of one used to issuing military-style orders.

Those were the kind of orders to which Gerald Quine was accustomed, and which Katina Plastridas obeyed. But obeyed only if they did not conflict with her primary task—the identification of anything, alien or domestic, which threatened the well-being of the United States. She had no idea of how her present quarry was a threat to the US, nor why she had been given the temporary identity of an FBI agent. During her five years in the Special Service she

had seldom known why she had been ordered
to do whatever it was she had been sent to do.

For as far back as she could remember Katina
had been fascinated by hidden things and secret meanings. She had enjoyed solving puz-
zles and probing mysteries, not for her own
advantage but for the inherent satisfaction of
discovering secrets. When she was a self-
confident freshman in Psych I, examining her
own motivations, she diagnosed herself as having a suppressed fear of hidden threats, which
emerged as a need to know everything going on
around her. In Psych IV, during her final year
at Wellesley, she reclassified her weakness as
simple curiosity, a minor obsession. In that
year she also took Cryptology, Theories of
Mysticism, Computer Programming, and Alien
Societies. She graduated Cum Magna Laude.

She also became the first Intercollegiate Womens Fencing Champion (Sabre), a title she acquired as a result of her relish for forcing an
Authority to show the real intent beneath the
wording of a regulation. An athletic girl with a
shorter reaction time, stronger arm muscles,
and acuter perceptions than most other young
women of her age, she had taken up fencing as
a sport, more because of the mystique associated with the sword than interest in its use.
She had fenced for Wellesley with the only
weapon the International Fencing Association

then allowed women—the foil. She had also fallen in love with a young man who specialized in the sabre.

Katina was the kind of girl willing to do anything for her beloved and she had acted as his opponent in unofficial training sessions. After a couple of months she had started to beat him. That had ended their romance and left her with a useless skill. In the period of generalized anger common among discarded lovers she had threatened the Amateur Athletic Union and the Intercollegiate Athletic Association with suit under the Equal Rights Amendment unless they admitted women to the sabre class in competitive fencing. She ached to beat the bastard in open competition.

The AAU had stood firm but the IAA had given ground to the extent of initiating an Intercollegiate Womens Championship. At that time there had been only a few women trained in sabre, and Katina had acquired the title despite her loss of interest in the weapon. By then her fury at the swordsman had been swamped by her love for a clarinetist.

Challenged by the way that legal language shrouded law, she had gone to Harvard Law School, intending to pull off the shrouds and expose the corpse. She had again graduated with honors but was no longer sure what she wanted to do. Like other top graduates she had been invited to Washington to discuss opportunities in the Federal Service. Like most of them she had ignored the invitation.

Unlike the others she had been pursued by Washington and eventually, intrigued by hints of unusual careers, she had gone for an interview. That interview had led to a series of others, each more intensive and less specific than the last, until she had finally finished in an anonymous office on K Street where she had been asked if she was interested in the US Special Service.

She had never heard of it. What was it? What did it do?

Her anonymous interviewer had thereupon bound her with an oath of secrecy and told her that the existence of the Special Service was not generally known, but could offer her an outlet for her athletic, legal, and psychological talents. If she wanted to learn more she would have to serve a probationary period.

Attracted by her interviewer's promise of total immersion in secrecy, she had accepted his challenge. After six months of hard training she could not bear to waste her painfully acquired skills and had joined the Service.

Since then she had found herself masquerading as a member of various other Federal agencies, including Defense Intelligence, Central Intelligence, General (Alien) Intelligence,

National Security, the FBI, and as a Security Officer seconded to Unipol. At first she had assumed the job of the Special Service was to act as the secret supervisor of the other Federal services—the policing of the police. But her orders at the beginning of each operation were seldom specific and she had soon realized her role was more than that of an intragovernment spy. Whatever that role was she must have performed well for she had received six promotions in the next four years and now ranked well above Gerald Quine in the Federal pecking order, though he, of course, did not know it. She had no doubt that she did her job well, but still was not certain that the job consisted only of playing hunches.

This operation promised to be more intriguing than any of her previous assignments, for on all of those she had been the only fake in a team of genuine agents. Here the only genuine agent was Quine. Neither Doctor Bose nor Lester Sloan were what they pretended to be. Before she left for Greece she consulted the central Service computer which informed her that Doctor Alexander Selin Tanaka Bose was a Deputy Director-General of the United Nations. It denied knowledge of any Lester Sloan, in Washington or elsewhere. Armed with this information and the photograph of an unknown but obviously fascinating woman, Katina caught the next flight to Athens.

She reported back ten days later in the company of Quine and, as was her general strategy, she let Quine speak for both of them. "Miss Plastiras backtrailed from Athens. I picked up the scent at Dulles airport. We now know the suspect's identity."

"Suspect? She isn't a suspect. Not yet!" protested Bose.

"I'm sorry, Doctor. A slip of the tongue."

"Suspect is a common term in police work," Sludic interrupted, leaning forward. "Mister Quine, who is she?"

"She goes under the name of Ruth Bettina Adams, sir." Quine was obviously happier reporting directly to Sloan. "As you surmised, she is now in the continental United States."

"Good work, officer," said Sludic. "How did you manage to identify her so quickly?"

"Careful attention to detail. Most international airports routinely photograph all embarking passengers, and send the photos to Unipol Identification after the flight has arrived safely. Without name-identification, of course. It would be illegal to store the name with the picture when the subject does not know that he or she has been photographed."

"I thought it was illegal to take people's photographs without their consent?" objected Bose.

"It is legal to take anybody's photograph," explained Quine patiently. "So long as the picture taken is not published, used for illegal purposes, or to hold the person photographed up to ridicule. It is still highly illegal to hijack civilian aircraft as the Terronationalists have done on occasion. Now that all the usual identity checks have become so easy to circumvent, thanks to the Transit access regulations imposed on us by those bastard aliens, security organizations have to use non-obvious procedures." Quine showed his irritation with this obtuse little man. "While passengers may not know they are routinely photographed, those with nothing to hide have nothing to fear."

"I suppose not," said Bose, and sighed. "But if the identity's not filed how did you identify this woman from her photograph?"

"The airlines retain duplicates of passenger photographs in case there are credit problems or lawsuits arise from accidental injury or death. There have been a number of cases of insurance fraud in which the insured was not the passenger on an aircraft but somebody traveling unknowingly under the insured's name. I advise you never to accept the offer of a free ticket—"

"So you got her name from the airline?"

"Yes. And confirmed it by a photograph taken by the Athens police."

"The Athens police!" Bose exploded. "I told you not to involve any police force."

"The woman herself got the police involved," Katina cut in. "She knocked out a young man in the middle of the airport concourse."

"She did what?"

"Knocked a man cold. He pinched her bottom. She chopped him down. In front of two policemen."

"Good God! And they arrested her?"

"When he recovered they were both taken to the police station to find out whether either wished to charge the other. The police were intrigued by the fact that the man worked for airport security and was trained in unarmed combat. I was able to get her description from their records. She gave her age as twenty-eight, her nationality as a U.S. citizen, and her occupation as "lady of independent means." Her height is recorded as one hundred and seventy-one centimeters and her weight as fifty-eight kilograms. She refused to let them take any of her other measurements. In the end, as neither wished to charge the other with assault, they were released together. The suspect—I mean Ms Adams—then took the young man out to dinner."

"Took him out to dinner? After he'd pinched her?"

"I think Ms Adams had the welfare of the young man in mind. She spent most of dinner giving him good advice, in adequate but archaic Greek."

"Miss Plastiras, how do you know all this?" asked Sludic.

"I myself spent an evening with him, as I had previously spent an evening with one of the policemen who had observed the incident. Neither could stop talking about her. To quote the young man's words: 'She has bruised my neck and broken my heart!' After dinner she allowed him to escort her to the boat for Mytelene."

Sludic was studying Katina with interest, Bose with alarm. "Is this your usual method of obtaining information?" asked Sludic.

"Obtaining information requires many different techniques. Most people give it more readily over a glass of wine and a good meal."

"You left Ms Adams on Mytelene," Bose said hastily. "That's a Greek island," he explained to Sludic.

"Where burning Sappho loved and sung," quoted the Marshal.

Bose stared at hearing an Auld quote Byron, Quine did not know he was quoting, and Katina continued as though she had not heard him.

"She stayed for three days in Lesbos, the largest town on Mytelene, acting like a typical tourist. She then went to Chios where she took a ferry to Psara, some eighteen kilometers from Chios. She stayed two nights on Psara, a small and rocky island with only one hotel. The proprietor remembered her as a woman of great beauty and commented particularly on her Titian hair."

"Hair color is not a good identifier," remarked Quine, patently annoyed at having lost the stage to a woman who was, moreover, his junior. "Fugitives often dye or cut their hair."

"It is impossible to dye hair Titian!" Katina glanced at her male colleague, and Quine's lips thinned. "The Titian effect is due to each hair having a different shade, ranging from gold to deep auburn. As it is not practical to dye each hair separately it is not possible to reproduce a true Titian. Everyone who saw Ms Adams agrees on the color of her hair. Moreover the Athens police photograph when examined microscopically shows the separate hairs having different colors."

"But if she wanted to disguise herself she could easily change her hair color, could she not?" asked Sludic.

"She could. But until after she had left Psara she made no attempt to disguise herself or cover her trail. While she was on Psara she even took a lover."

"What?" Bose was on his feet and even Sludic showed surprise.

"She took a lover," repeated Katina, as astonished by their reactions as they were at her statement. "She's single and in the sexually active age group."

Bose sat down slowly. "Who?"

"A young professor from Cornell named Peter Ward. He was staying in the hotel. The Proprietor called it a chance meeting and a temporary liaison. The kind of passing affair common between tourists of different sexes when traveling alone. Or between tourists of the same sex, for that matter."

Quine's lips thinned again. Bose looked uncomfortable. "Professor of what?"

"Classics. He has stayed at that hotel before. He usually spends a couple of weeks among the Greek islands every spring and fall."

"How long did this liaison last?"

"A single night. They left on the ferry the next afternoon after spending the day together somewhere up on the hillside. They parted affectionately when they reached Athens. I was unable to trace Ms Adams any further."

"Where is this Professor Ward now?"

"Back at Cornell," said Quine. "I have already checked his record. He is—well—he has never come to the attention of any police force. He seems a harmless academic."

"He is well regarded at the Classical Institute in Athens," added Katina. "His special field is Aeolic Greek."

Bose was still stunned by the news that this alien had taken a human lover. "Where is Miss Adams now?"

"I don't know where she is at the moment, Doctor. But I have her home address. She owns a house in Maryland, near Frederick. She paid over two million for it five years ago—without a mortgage. She appears to be a wealthy woman, but I have not yet uncovered the source of her wealth. She employs a housekeeper and a gardener to look after her house; the same couple have worked for her since she bought it. She only returns to it at irregular intervals. Our agents are watching it."

"For the time being—only watch it," said Sludic. "I don't want Miss Adams to know that she is under surveillance."

"That's Alia all right," said the Marshal, studying the woman with the furious expression and the glorious hair who stared up at them from the Athens police photograph. "She not only looks like Alia. Her physical reaction to sudden assault is typical of Alia."

"I can't believe she's not human," said Bose. "How could an alien have sex with a man?"

"I cannot pretend to understand the sexual responses of many races in the Arm. Those of humans are among the more bizarre, judging by the immense literature you have on the subject. But I agree that Alia has somehow acquired or developed a body which resembles a human female more closely than I had thought."

"It's not just her body. It's her behavior."

"I am finding that it is not so difficult to mimic human behavior."

"Have you tried taking a human to bed yet?"

Sludic shuddered. "That is something I shall never attempt! However Alia seems to have done so. From my study of the literature and from waching your pornographic television channel, human sexual interactions seem so diverse that a being with only limited human attributes might suit a certain type of man. Alia might never have taken off her clothes."

"Not a healthy young man like this Peter Ward seems to be," objected Bose.

"We must find out. And for that we must interview him."

"Interview him? Us?" Bose had not expected to become personally involved in the quest for Alia, and did not relish the prospect.

"Nobody but ourselves knows enough about Alia to ask the appropriate questions."

"But we can't just walk in on this Professor and ask him if Ruth Adams was a—" Bose searched for a suitable phrase. "If she was a good lay!"

"Your ingenuity, Alex, should produce an adequate reason for a meeting with Peter Ward. And I suspect he will hardly be able to restrain himself from talking about Alia if we give him the slightest excuse. That is the effect she has on most individuals of most races."

VI

The doorbell rang and Peter cursed. It was now six weeks since he and Thalia had parted on the dockside at Piraeus and she had promised to get in touch with him within three months. He was spending most of his free time in his apartment, discouraging visitors and waiting for her to call. He wanted to be alone when she did.

He was also writing poetry. As soon as he had arrived back in Ithaca he had taken her advice, selected some of the better translations of Sappho, added a few of his own verses for luck, and mailed the lot to the Cultural Attaché at the Auld Embassy. The answer, from "The Century Publishing Co.," had been both prompt and encouraging, a combination which had never crowned any of his previous efforts. The anonymous editor had thanked him for his submission, returned most of the translations but kept Shelley's and two of his own. And the letter had been unique in that it had been accompanied by a modest check for what the editor called a "finder's fee," plus a considerably larger one as advanced royalties for himself as an author. The total was the equivalent of a month's salary for an assistant professor, and there might be more to come should the edition of "Terran Poets," in which his work would be included, prove a commercial success.

The fact that somebody, alien or human, had actually paid him for his poetry was a reward beyond dollars; his highest previous payment had been a year's free subscription to the magazine concerned. (Several other magazines had demanded that he take out subscriptions before they'd publish his poems.) The check was solid encouragement to produce more. On the table was his only communication from Thalia, the words of the extra verses she had sung in "Hymn to Aphrodite." Now that he had had a chance to study them he was certain they were genuine Sappho, and was determined to give them the translation they deserved. The possibility that Sappho would sing among the stars with his voice was the ultimate inspiration.

So when the bell rang he chewed the end of his pen and waited for the uninvited caller to go away. When it sounded a second time he was seized by the wild hope that Thalia might be arriving in person and bounded from his chair to the front door with his heart in his mouth. Then he opened the door to find two men, one short and dark, the other tall and fair, standing outside.

"My name is Doctor Bose," said the short one. "You were expecting somebody else?"

"Yes—er—not exactly," said Peter, his disappointment clear on his face.

"We're looking for Professor Peter Ward, the celebrated classical scholar."

"That's me," admitted Peter, his annoyance at the interruption momentarily swamped by the pleasure of hearing himself described as a celebrated classical scholar.

"I am an historian with the United Nations," explained Doctor Bose. "A medical historian." Which was not entirely untrue. He was writing a history of the World Health Organization since the arrival of the aliens. It included the story of his own first encounter with them and therefore would not be published until many years after his death.

"Yes?" said Peter somewhat more warmly,

but without moving aside or inviting his visitors into his apartment.

Bose interpreted Peter's hesitation as suspicion and produced the UN identity card he had had specially prepared. Peter waved it aside, but still did not invite them in. Ambivalence is the occupational disease of academics.

"I am visiting Cornell to use the facilities of your splendid library," Bose continued, laboring more as the going got heavier. He was unused to lying and resented Sludic's avoiding the necessity by letting Bose lie for him.

"The medical library's at the Medical School in New York City," said Peter.

"My present interest is in preclassical Greek medicine," said Bose hastily. 'I have several excerpts from that period for which my translations seem inadequate. Most of the scholars whom I consulted referred me to you as the authority on preclassical Greek in this part of the United States."

Peter's attitude warmed. The Chairman of Classics would go ape if he heard his junior colleague referred to as the leading authority in the Chairman's own area. "You want me to look at them?"

"If you would be so kind." Bose began a slow fumble in his briefcase.

"Come on in," said Peter, touched by the sight of this elderly scholar's typical confusion.

"Thank you. Thank you indeed!" said Bose, closing his briefcase. "May I introduce my friend Doctor Sloan. He is traveling with me, but his is quite a different field of endeavor. Do you mind if he sits down while we talk?"

"If he can stand the chaos and find somewhere to sit," said Peter, ushering the pair into the living room. He used a five-day cycle for his housekeeping, letting crockery, garbage, linen, and newspapers accumulate for five days then cleaning up on the sixth. This was the fifth day of the cycle. He dumped books from the couch and waved his guests to a seat.

Sludic had already taken one at the table and was now studying an enlarged photograph of Thalia which was smiling at them from among a cluster of dirty dishes. Bose, after one quick glance at the picture, sat down on the couch, rummaged through his brief-case, and produced several pages of hand-written Greek. "These are the passages on which I'd like your opinion."

Peter glanced at them, took the bait, sat down, and began to read. Sludic picked up the poem which Peter had been composing.

"I can't identify this off-hand," said Peter presently. "It looks like something from the Hippocratic writers, the medical authorities grouped under the name of Hippocrates, but written in the Aeolic Greek that was used—"

He stopped and studied the pages more intently. "What this looks like to me is an attempt by somebody to translate the Ionic Greek of Hippocrates into the Aeolic. I can't imagine why!"

As that is exactly what a protesting linguist on the staff of the United Nations had attempted to do, Bose tried to look pleased while feeling ashamed. "Aeolic Greek? That was the dialect used by Alcaeus, was it not?"

"Alcaeus, Sappho, Anacreon—it was the Greek spoken by the greatest lyric poets who ever lived!" said Peter with the enthusiasm of the fanatic. "It had been absorbed into Ionic by the time of Hippocrates." He stared thoughtfully at the manuscript. "Though there was a tendency for later lyricists to try writing in Aeolic—the way Victorian poets used archaic English in attempts to be sentimentally medieval."

"I see you are a poet yourself, Doctor Ward," said Sludic from his seat at the table. "And an excellent poet too, judging by this sample." He held up the draft on which Peter had been working.

Peter jumped to his feet in anger and embarrassment. This stranger had had the effrontery to poke through his papers! Then pride swamped his annoyance. "I write a bit of poetry," he admitted.

"I am no connoisseur of verse," said Sludic.

"But I know what I like. And I like this! I like it very much."

"I haven't started to polish it yet," said Peter, pleased but protesting.

"Don't overpolish it," advised Sludic, speaking with all the authority of a Marshal. "This has a fine rhythm." He tapped his toe to demonstrate. "I didn't know there was still anybody writing the kind of English verse I enjoy. So yours is quite a find for me, Doctor Ward."

Bose had been listening to Sludic with growing horror. The Marshal's fulsome praise would blow their cover. The young man would see through the whole façade, throw them out as impostors, and doubtless give Alia an account of the incident. She would recognize Sloan as Sludic and their whole plan would be shattered.

He had underestimated the capacity of poets for praise. Peter did not interpret Sludic's words as fulsome; to him they were the comments of an acute critic, sensitive to the virtues of his verse. "You like it? You really like it?"

"Indeed I do!" Sludic put the poem down among the used coffee mugs. "I hope you are writing more with the same powerful rhythm." He indicated the photograph of Alia. "Is this beautiful lady the source of your inspiration?"

"In a way." Peter was both embarrassed and

pleased by the perspicacity of this stranger. "I met her in Greece during spring." The temptation of a lover to talk about his beloved is as strong as that of a scholar to discuss his subject or of a poet to recite his poetry. "I'm hoping to see her again soon." To disguise his excitement at the prospect he went into the kitchen and fixed three large Scotches without asking his guests their preference. He came back, handed a glass to Sludic, a glass to Bose, and took a gulp of his own. He could not deny himself the pleasure of talking about the woman who filled his thoughts. "Yes—she's the one who encouraged me."

"Her face shows intelligence as well as beauty. An unusual face!"

Bose, who had been flabbergasted by the ready way that Peter was swallowing Sludic's overripe praise, injected a remark to the effect that all women were unusual.

"They're all a bit weird," agreed Peter. He took Thalia's photograph from the Marshal and sank down on the couch, the photograph in one hand, his whisky in the other. "But she's—well—numinous! The most beautiful woman I've ever seen." He sat adoring the picture and sipping the whisky. "She's American. I'm hoping to see her again when she gets back to the States."

"Where is she now?"

Peter shrugged. "Wish I knew!" And he launched into a panegryic on her beauty, finally producing two sonnets he had dedicated to her but which she had not yet seen because he didn't know where to mail them. "Do you think she'll like them? Are they good enough to show her?"

"They'll make her a very proud young lady," pronounced Sludic.

Peter offered to pour his guests another Scotch and when they refused he poured one for himself. He reread his own poems, stared at Thalia's picture, and then returned to describing her sensitivity, intelligence, and beauty. He was the kind of man who would never intentionally betray a lady's reputation, even in an age when most of his female contemporaries would regard a description of their skill in bed as a compliment rather than a betrayal. But by the time he had meandered on for half an hour, fortified by Scotch and encouraged by Sludic, Bose had a vivid picture of Alia's physical and behavioral characteristics. The picture of a decisive woman with the face of a goddess, hair beautiful beyond belief, the figure of an athlete, the taste of a connoisseur, and the brains of a genius. "There's something mystical about her. An aura I can't describe in prose." He swirled the whisky in his glass. "God—I hope I see her again!"

He was so much the image of the distraught lover that Bose's heart was touched. He gripped Peter's shoulder and said he was sure he would. Then, claiming they had a plane to catch, they left the lovelorn young man to drink alone.

"Greek Lyric Poets—A Critical Evaluation" was a course given by the Chairman of Classics to a handful of summer students seeking sufficient credits to graduate at the Fall Convocation. That summer the Chairman was away and the load fell on his junior—Peter Ward.

He approached the task with loathing. Not only did it interfere with his own work, it promised to destroy any liking for lyric verse among the students. The required text was the Chairman's scholarly dissection of lines which poets "tossing on their beds, rhymed out in love's despair/ To flatter Beauty's ignorant ear." After reading his Chairman's translations (most students now knew little Latin and less Greek), Peter took the dangerous step of substituting his own.

That step carried him further than he had intended. By introducing his own translations he also injected his own enthusiasms into a course designed to teach criticism rather than encourage appreciation. Peter quoted Sappho to the class with unacademic fervor, altering the accepted pronunciation and syntax on the basis of unreferenced "recent discoveries."

The size of the class increased as the course progressed; unregistered students came to hear his lectures. Among them was a young woman with black hair who sat silent at the back of the room, but whose brightened eyes showed the response which the sapphics were evoking. Other members of the department also started to drift in, intrigued by this unusual student interest in an area of their scholarship. Some were as fascinated as the students to hear a poet interpreting a poet, others were as disapproving as the Chairman would be at Peter's liberal transformation of Aeolic lyrics into formal English verse. The Chairman would certainly hear both opinions on his return. Peter was too pleased by the students' reception of his efforts to worry, as yet, about the old scholar's probable reaction.

Students and colleagues started to stay after his lectures to offer comments or ask questions. They also began to send him notes. He was working his way through a pile of those one July morning when he came on a sheet bearing Leonard's translation of Sappho's lovely lines: *"The Moon and seven Pleiades have set; / It is the midnight now, the hours go by; / And still I'm lying on my bed alone."* Underneath was scribbled, "The following are of doubtful validity, but might interest you," followed by an indecipherable signature and three lines in Greek.

Casually Peter translated the Greek, looked at what he had written, and laughed. The lines were not only fake, they included anachronisms that showed them recent. "Sad Electra's poet" was a phrase used by Milton with reference to Euripedes, and Sappho was dead long before Euripedes and Milton were born. "Son of Semele" was Alcaeus' name for Dionysus, the wine god. The source of "well-spiced beans" he couldn't place. Sounded like chili! And the whole effect was banal. He reread his translation. *"But when the sun's near noon, I will invoke / The voice of Sad Electra. Seek you out / Among the flowing wine and well-spiced beans / Served by the portly Son of Semele."*

Either a fraud or a hoax. But in impeccable Aeolic! The Chairman was the only other classicist at Cornell capable of composing in that dialect. He would never have descended to perpetrating such nonsense. Nor could he—he was in Tokyo.

Peter jumped to his feet, upsetting his coffee. Thalia, of course! He mopped coffee from his slacks while he attacked the riddle. Why send a message in this bizarre form? Because she didn't want anybody else to understand what she was saying? The voice of sad Electra? Telephone or radio. Son of Selene? Well-spiced beans? Sonny's Grill was a popular student hang-out, near the campus, run by a large fat man, specializing in chili! The message meant that she'd be phoning him there. Why not his office or apartment? Why the secrecy? Perhaps Pirenne's thugs were after her again. Perhaps it was her liking for mystery. Or a test of his perspicacity?

Whatever her reason, she was telling him to start eating lunch around midday in Sonny's Grill. She would call him there. And there he would be—every day from now on.

VII

Quine sat facing them with the expression of a successful bounty-hunter. "I now have evidence that the woman calling herself Ruth Bettina Adams is an impostor, and has committed a Federal offence which would allow me to obtain a warrant for her arrest."

"I don't want her arrested on a technicality," said Bose, glancing uneasily at Sludic.

"This isn't a technicality, Doctor. I think this is a case of impersonation." Quine was glad to be finally faced with a genuine crime. He had assumed that their quarry was either a clever female con artist or, less likely, involved in some form of espionage. Basically just another woman crook. It bruised his professional pride that this Doctor Bose and his partner from Washington would not tell him what she'd done.

It was bruised again when Sludic snapped, "Mister Quine, gather information but nothing else, as yet. Now, tell us what you have discovered."

I checked with the Passport Office, (Quine said) and found they issued a passport to a Ruth Adams of Chicago seven years ago. They were still issuing passports then. Both the description and the photograph match the suspect's exactly. She had to produce her birth certificate before she could be issued with a passport, and her birthplace was recorded as Dan Meadows, West Virginia.

I personally went to Dan Meadows to interview her family and found the place to be an almost depopulated mountain village. None of her relatives were traceable. Her father was killed in an incident involving illicit liquor when she was a child and her mother died of cirrhosis of the liver two years ago. The reputation of both her parents and of the girl herself was unsavory. She ran away with a truck driver at sixteen and nobody in Dan Meadows had seen her since. There was a rumor that she was dead, but her mother had denied it vehemently.

The girl's mother had been living in poverty—welfare had not been sufficient to provide her with both a reasonable life-style and an unreasonable amount of liquor. Seven years ago, however, she began to receive a generous allowance from her daughter and that continued to her death. It probably contributed to her death, as she had been able to purchase all the liquor she wanted.

The Adamses are old West Virginian mountain stock. Black Irish with generations of inbreeding. Everybody I spoke to who remembered Ruth described her as having jet-black hair. I returned to Chicago. The address given on the passport application was an apartment block in an expensive district. The apartment guard remembered Miss Adams well and verified the suspect's picture was her.

Because of the rumor that the girl was dead, I put a trace on all hospital and coroner's records for any female Adams appearing in the years immediately prior to the passport application. I found Ruth Adams mentioned in connection with the death of a young woman. The deceased was not named Adams; she was only referred to as "Betty" in the records of the Cook County Hospital. The woman who brought her to the Emergency and who later identified the body called herself Ruth Adams.

I had hoped that we would be able to charge

the suspect with murder, but unfortunately there is not sufficient evidence to support such a charge. This Betty had been in the Emergency on a number of previous occasions. The diagnoses listed were attempted suicide, drug overdosage, and lacerations. Lacerations inflicted either by her pimp or by dissatisfied customers. Betty was a prostitute. An unsuccessful prostitute. The woman who brought her in stated she had known her for some time, had rescued her before, but on this occasion had found her too late. Hospital records confirm this.

Those records also indicate Betty had black hair. The death certificate gives the cause of death as aspiration pneumonia consequent on barbiturate overdosage and alcohol intoxication. I applied to have the body exhumed, only to discover that it had been released to the so-called Ruth Adams for burial after the inquest. The Coroner had been happy to save the County the cost as no relatives had come forward. The so-called Ruth Adams gave the deceased a respectable funeral—and had her cremated!

I identified and interrogated the pimp. He insisted that all he had known about Betty was that she was a hill-billy who cheated, drank, and drugged. When pressed he remembered a woman with red hair who had given Betty money and taken her to the hospital twice. He identified the photo of the suspect as the red-haired woman concerned. On closer interrogation he admitted that the woman had warned him to leave Betty alone, and had slapped him around when he had failed to do so. Under further pressure he finally admitted that she had come and broken both his arms after Betty died.

Quine closed his notebook and waited for his two seniors to draw the obvious conclusion. The Doctor was staring at him in horror. "Broke both his arms? Good God!"

"The pimp was not a muscular person, Doctor."

"You think that the red-haired woman took the identity of Ruth Adams after Betty, the real Miss Adams, died?" asked the man from Washington.

"That is suggested by the circumstantial evidence, sir. The sudden allowance which Mrs. Adams began to receive shortly afterward supports this. During a follow-up investigation of Dan Meadows I discovered that Mrs. Adams had a visitor from the city a few days after Betty's cremation. It was following that visit that she vehemently denied rumors of her daughter's death."

"Who—who signed the passport application?" asked Dr. Bose.

"Her bank manager who knew her only as a client. And the lawyer who acted for her in the purchase and sale of her apartment. Neither had known her for more than a couple of years. And neither had taken the application very seriously. Even then most people were not bothering to obtain passports before traveling abroad. An alien "Admission-to-Transit" is easy to get, costs nothing, and no customs or immigration official dares to delay anybody presenting one of the damned things."

"Then why should the suspect have bothered to get one?"

Quine shrugged. "For some people to get a passport and travel under it used to be a patriotic gesture. I myself hold a United States passport. I refuse to handle one of those damned alien cards!" He held back his anger. "In the case of the suspect I suggest she was misusing it as a means of establishing her false identity."

Bose was pulling nervously at the little finger of his left hand. "But as passports are no longer issued why is a false declaration cause to arrest her?"

"Making a false statement to any department of the Federal Government is sufficiently serious for me to take her in for questioning." Quine paused. "Within twenty-four hours of detaining her I can have sufficient evidence for a warrant."

An expression of loathing passed across Bose's face. The reports of Amnesty International had grown grimmer year by year as Governments lost their public means of enforcing law and order, and turned increasingly to clandestine methods.

"Do not arrest her!" snapped Sludic. "Do nothing to let her suspect she is under observation."

"As you wish, sir," said Quine, slipping his notebook into his pocket and standing up. He was losing his respect for the fellow from Washington and had never had much for the Doctor. "We have her house in Maryland under constant observation and I will inform you immediately she returns. If she does return."

"And Professor Ward, you have him under observation?"

"Miss Plastiras is shadowing the Professor. She has not contacted me. I understand you authorized her to act independently." Quine showed his resentment at having his seniority ignored.

"We did," said Sludic. He also was regarding Quine with dislike. "That will be all for now."

"Where is Miss Plastiras?" asked Bose.

Quine, who had started for the door, stopped and turned. "She has not informed me of her plans or her whereabouts."

"If she does contact you, tell her to telephone me."

Quine nodded, and had reached the door when he was again stopped, this time by the bastard from Washington. 'Order your agents to be very discreet. We are hunting a fugitive of exceptional intelligence."

Quine did not even nod but escaped through the door. He disliked being criticised. He detested being patronized.

"This confirms that Ruth Adams is Alia." Sludic put the passport photograph down on the desk. "The maneuvers we have heard described are typical of Alia. Quine has done well to trace her."

"I can't believe she's not human," said Bose slowly. "How could an alien have a sexual encounter with a man? Ward's infatuated with her."

Sludic looked up from the picture. "I will now agree that Alia either by nature or by aquisition has a body resembling that of a human female more closely than I had thought."

"It's not only her body. It's the humanity of her actions. She did look after that poor girl. She did try to prevent her death, even if she took advantage of it after she had died. And she did avenge it."

"Common humanity is not the prerogative

of human beings! But even if Alia's anatomy proves human, the fact remains that she is an alien unlawfully on Earth. And that I was hunting her long before the existence of Earth was known."

"Then there must be humans in other parts of the Cluster," insisted Bose.

"That is unlikely. Any hominoid race within the frontiers of civilization or on the fringe would certainly have forced themselves upon our attention long ago. You are a race which, once contacted, cannot be ignored!"

Coming from a Galactic Marshal that was close to a compliment. Bose asked, "What now? Quine wants to arrest and interrogate her."

"And you do not welcome that solution?"

"I don't like the idea of Quine having a free hand in the interrogation of a woman."

"Would you feel the same repugnance were she not a woman but an alien?"

"Yes! Damnation! Yes—I would!" Bose jumped to his feet. "Man—woman—child—alien of any variety! Any intellectual being who can suffer. Any creature that can suffer, for that matter." He unclenched his fists and went back to his chair. "What if I tell you to go to hell? That Alia's human and under my protection?"

"In the face of the evidence I have produced regarding the length of time I have been hunt-

ing her, I would consider you biased beyond
the ability to judge. Or resolved to frustrate
the Transit Authority."

"What the devil has she done that's made
you hunt her for so long?"

"Most of her offenses have been minor. It is
not so much what she has done that justifies
my seizing her. It's what she knows." Sludic
paused, as though he had made a confession
which had burdened his conscience for a long
time. "Alex, you are now my friend. But duty
takes precedence over even friendship. If you
do not have her arrested and handed over to
me when I order it, I will have no choice but to
start reducing the supplies of electrical energy
to North America. You would not long remain
in a position to refuse to arrest her. Your
Director-General would transfer you. Perhaps
even have you held incommunicado while
Quine arrests her and surrenders her to me."

Bose knew that to be true. The rulers of the
world might detest the idea of anyone who
even looked like a woman being surrendered to
the aliens. But they would detest even more
the political reactions of a people who were
losing accustomed conveniences, and who would
never be allowed to know the reason.

Defeated, he slumped back into his chair.
"When and if she goes to her house in Maryland Quine will have her cornered. All right,

I'll go with him when the time comes. But I insist you come with me."

"Why do you insist, Alex?"

"Because you're a Marshal. You claim Alia can be very dangerous. I've no idea how. But you know. Now that you look and talk like a man—act like one! You've no excuse for dodging the dirty job of arresting her!"

Sludic's face went cold. The insult touched his Auld pride. Bose glimpsed the ruthless power he might release if roused. Then the Marshal relaxed and nodded. "You are right Alex. It is a prospect I detest more than you can understand. But it is my duty."

Bose walked to the bookshelves. He returned with a leather-bound volume. "Sada—read this. *Les Miserables* by Victor Hugo. There's a character in it whom you may find sympathetic. His name is Javert."

VIII

Katina Plastiras listened with half an ear to the arguments swirling about her. With the other half she listened to the bug she had planted on Peter Ward. He was lunching alone at a table on the far side of Sonny's Grill; the fact that he had emerged from his apartment to eat at this student hang-out suggested some kind of a rendez-vous. With Ruth Adams, she hoped.

She herself was another long-haired graduate student drinking beer and analyzing the archaic attitudes of the School of Graduate Studies. In a black sweatshirt and faded jeans she was playing a role that had been her life only a few years before. Had she followed it she might have become another penurious Assistant Professor, like the one she was shadowing. Instead, she was watching him and wondering what the hell she was supposed to be doing.

The Service had asked no questions when she had requisitioned an advance microbug, and had only answered hers with the usual, "You're doing fine! Stay with it and report whatever seems important." That was after Bose and Sloan had detached her from Quine, told her to follow her own intuition.

Her intuition had told her to follow Peter Ward. From what she had learned on Psara, from Bose's description of his visit to the Professor's apartment, from his present air of alarmed hope, she was sure that a transient romance between two tourists had exploded into a mutual infatuation. Sooner or later Ruth Adams would contact Peter—Katina hoped sooner. Graduate student gossip which had been fascinating in the past had become puerile and boring with the years. She followed the conversation at her table, listened to the sounds of Peter eating chili, and sipped her beer. Drinking without imbibing, listening without hearing, arguing without involvement—skills taught her by the Service.

"Doctor Ward!" the bartender bellowed. "It's for you, doc!" He jerked his thumb toward the telephone. "Sounds like a patient. Says it's urgent!" The last for the benefit of the other customers. Sonny catered to the appetites of students but did not encourage incoming calls.

Peter jumped to his feet and pushed through the crush as if he were indeed a physician expecting a call. He had been expecting a call all right, but not from a patient. Katina concentrated on the bug and caught only a few words when he picked up the phone, but they were enough to confirm her hunch. He had come to Sonny's for Ruth Adams to make contact.

"Ward here . . . Thalia? Is that you? . . . A mob all round me . . . Yes . . . Okay . . . A cab? . . . Pick me up? . . . I'll wait . . . Yes, I'll keep my eyes open! Listen—" The caller must have hung up for Peter hung up too and looked round the crowded Grill. Then he pushed a bill across the bar, abandoned his chili, left his change, and charged for the street. Katina eased from the group around her table and followed him.

He was standing on the sidewalk, looking up and down College; then he looked round, as though suddenly remembering he had been told to make sure he wasn't being followed. Katina merged with the students queuing to eat the cheapest meal within reach of the Cornell campus. When a cab pulled into the curb Peter exchanged some brief remarks with the driver, then jumped in beside him. Just a cab sent to pick up a fare. She ran to her battered Ford, parked farther up the street. A black Buick containing three men pulled out ahead of her. She let the cab and the Buick get well down College before she followed. The microbug would only relay Peter's words a few dozen meters, but the tracker in her Ford could read its range and bearing for several kilometers.

The cab turned right on Mitchell. The Buick did the same. The two cars went down the steep hill into Ithaca with the Buick a hundred meters back. They crawled through the town along Cayuga, and both took Route 89 out of it. By then Katina no longer doubted that Peter had picked up another tail besides herself. And she was fairly confident that neither knew she was astern of both.

She was not especially surprised to find some other agency besides the FBI was interested in Ruth Adams. If her own Service was interested, then Ruth Adams was interesting. And Doctor Bose was top-brass at the UN so Unipol was involved. And if Unipol was involved a lot of national agencies were informed. UN Security was riddled with double-loyalties.

Sloan? He was top-brass in something. He spoke like a man used to being obeyed. And his last words to her had been, "Miss Plastiras, if you intercept Miss Adams, follow her and phone us. But, until we take over, your prime duty is to protect her!" From what? Sloan had been vague.

Perhaps from the men in the Buick. She had only glimpsed them, but they had not looked like officers from any respectable Agency. More like hired hit men. But such people were sometimes used by respectable agencies for jobs too sordid for their own operators. Katina felt her pulse starting to pound, tasted the excitement on her tongue.

The Buick was having no difficulty in following the cab. Katina's suspicions stirred. Peter had evidently been warned to look out for tails, yet the cab pickup had been a crude maneuver for a woman who had disappeared so effectively in Athens. She closed on the bug, then dropped back again when, on the hill beyond Ithaca, she saw the Buick still between her and her target.

Route 89 climbed into open country above the lake. The Buick started to close on the cab. Were the men in it preparing to snatch Peter? Poor tactics if they were after the woman. But Katina was closing on the Buick when the cab turned off the highway and down a lane between smart white fences to a group of manicured buildings ranged round a large barn. The notice by the gateway warned, "Ithaca Hunt

Club—Members Only." Then enticed, "Riding Lessons Available by Arrangement."

The Buick had slowed as the cab turned, then gone past the entrance to the lane. Katina swung in as though the Club had been her goal all the time. The parking lot was half-filled. She hid the Ford behind a Cadillac, then strolled to the stableyard and took cover behind the barn. Peter had paid off the cab and was staring toward the stables, conspicuously incongruous in these horsey surroundings.

A woman came cantering from the paddock, leading a saddled mare, Katina did not need Peter's excited shout to know this was the woman she had to watch and protect. And even in her satisfaction at having caught up with her quarry, she felt a spasm of jealousy. Ruth Adams was even more beautiful than her picture. No photograph can reflect the glory of Titian hair gleaming in the sunlight. No policeman's words could describe the cool assurance of the woman astride the roan gelding; a woman whose mere presence evoked interest—let alone whatever she had done to rouse that of the UN and the FBI.

Peter had run toward her, waving and shouting. Her smile was warm, but her words were curt. "Climb aboard and let's go."

Katina almost clapped her hands at the ingenuity of the maneuver. Peter scrambled up onto the mare in a way that suggested he had ridden horses, but not often. The woman swung her roan back toward the paddock and kicked it into a trot just as the Buick came down the lane and turned into the yard.

Katina seized a pitchfork and began shifting a pile of stable manure as the three men tumbled from the Buick. One ran after the two riders; the others stood cursing. Katina continued to shift manure while studying the three men. Hired guns—no doubt about that!

The one who had run into the paddock stopped to watch the two riders cantering down a trail toward the woods. Pursuit on foot was useless; pursuit by car was impossible. He returned to join his two companions and the three stood studying maps, trying to guess where the riders would emerge. By the time they had decided Katina was sweating and the manure was mostly moved.

The Buick roared out onto the highway and she ran to her Ford. The tracker showed the pair were still riding through the woods. The chances of intercepting them without its aid would be slim. The whole area was a network of riding trails and underbrush. She began to cruise leisurely along side roads, keeping Peter's blip in view on the screen.

Professional hit-men usually follow their calling in urban jungles rather than rural woodlands, and they hunt men and women in automobiles rather than on horseback. Ruth Adams probably had a car waiting at the end of one of the many trails. Katina was still admiring her ingenuity when, driving slowly down a dirt road, she saw a blue Jaguar parked in a field by the woods with a stable-hand leaning on the hood, smoking a cigarette. Her admiration for Ruth Adams evaporated. The man was obviously waiting for the car's owner to arrive and was visible for miles.

Katina turned up a lane, parked, and watched the screen of the tracker. The blip showing Peter's progress came closer and then stopped. The riders had evidently arrived at the car. She sat tense, silently urging them to get going before the searching Buick arrived, cursing them for dawdling. She relaxed when the blip started to move again and the Jaguar went past the end of the lane. Then she resumed cursing as, moments later, the Buick followed. The lovers had lingered too long.

She started her Ford and went after them, still lying well back, wondering if she should call for help. But her pride was at issue as well as her orders not to involve anybody else in the hunt unless absolutely necessary. As yet, it was not necessary. She was certain that the three men in the Buick did not know they were being trailed.

Ruth Adams was driving as though she did not even suspect such a thing. Yet she had glanced toward the Buick when it had arrived in the yard, and had looked back when she had cantered toward the woods. The arrival of Peter must have blown her wits! The pair in the Jaguar were probably already exploring each other as they dawdled westward along Route 79. Katina, at the rear of the procession, felt another spasm of jealousy for the Titian-haired beauty ahead.

The traffic became heavier as they went through Mecklenburg, the road dipping and climbing across the valleys and hills between the Finger Lakes. She glimpsed the Jaguar cresting the hills ahead, now with a dozen cars between it and the Buick. She was wondering why there were so many on this quiet by-way when she saw a notice nailed to a tree, announcing a hill-climb at Watkins Glen. They had joined a stream of auto enthusiasts, heading for a weekend of vicarious thrills and associated pleasures.

As they approached the Glen more cars poured in along converging highways and the traffic slowed to a crawl. The Buick was attempting to jump the queues and the arriving drivers were in no mood to be jumped. An altercation developed at the next crossroads where the Buick had bumped a panel truck heavily ornamented with dragons and naked women. Its driver looked as though he was about to mix it up with the driver of the Buick. The hit-men were in alien territory and their reactions were inappropriate. Katina saw three hard and angry faces as she eased past.

The Jaguar was now far ahead, but not far enough. Katina was horrified to find it parked outside a room in a large rambling motel, a collection of single-story buildings surrounded by acres of concrete parking lot. There was no sign of the car's occupants. The pair were evidently so hungry to get into bed that they were now ignoring elementary precautions.

She parked some way from it and went to book a room for herself, taking up her role as covert bodyguard. The office and the central bar-restaurant complex was seething with automobile enthusiasts, already warming up for their weekend carouse. She pushed through the mob at the desk and told the clerk she wanted Room 406, the one opposite where the lovers were parked.

"No vacancies!" The clerk smirked. "Been booked solid for days!" Had Ruth Adams prepared her love nest days before?

Katina went around the desk and into the Manager's office. "You want this funkhouse searched? Or do I get Room 406?" She showed one of her badges.

The Manager stopped shouting, shot out to the desk, and hissed at the clerk, "Courtesy booking! No charge!" He thrust the room key at her. "No bust, officer! Not tonight. This mob'll take the place apart if you try!"

"Stay cool. Keep quiet. No bust." She took the key. "Real quiet. You understand?"

The Manager nodded, mopping his face, and watched Katina start toward her Ford. Then she saw a State Police cruiser parked on the shoulder of the highway and changed direction. Partly to further impress the Manager, partly to get a backup. The Trooper looked like a helpful young man.

He smiled at the long-haired young woman smelling of horse manure. "Need help, ma'am?"

"Yes." She showed her FBI badge and shut off his smile. Police everywhere had learned that it paid to help a Federal Agent and it hurt to thwart one. Men like Quine made sure of that. They also made the Agency unpopular. Rather too similar to the Greek Political Police of her father's day for Katina's taste, but useful on occasions like this. "Stay near the motel, but not on display. Monitor band 79. Come if I call."

"I'm on patrol—"

"You still are. Near here. Log it as 'Supporting Federal Agent.' Your Sergeant'll know enough not to ask questions. Have your dispatcher ring the Agency. Check me out—number against description." She showed her ID. "Does my face fit?"

He looked at the ID, then at her. "Sure does, ma'am!" His smile came back. "I'll hang close. You after something bigger than pushers on horseback?"

"Something hotter. Too hot for your report. Federal security. If I call—come fast!"

"Sure will! But I go off duty at ten."

"You go off duty when I say. Maybe around ten tomorrow." She pushed back her hair. "What's your name? Jim? I'm Katina. No last names, eh?" She found herself smiling. "Sorry to wreck your evening, but I may need backup and I've no time to call in the cavalry!"

He smiled back. "Pleased to be of help, ma'am." He touched his hat and pulled out onto the highway. Katina looked after him, sighed, then went to her Ford for her kit.

She had just reached her room when the Buick arrived. She eased back the curtain from her window and watched it circle the motel, slow as it passed the Jaguar, then park farther along. Two of the three in it walked toward the office. Katina judged she had time for a shower. She stank of stables.

She watched the Buick as she dried herself off. This Ruth Adams was being hunted not only by the Agency but by some organization which hired men like those three. She'd been lucky to spot them before they spotted her. They were concentrating on the woman. She must find out why. If she could snatch one she might. Or at least who he worked for. A professional hit man is no hero; he puts a high value on human life, his own higher than his victim's.

They wouldn't try anything until dark. She dressed and pulled the bed over to the window. Then she assembled her weapons. A pneumatic rifle loaded with paralyzer darts. A supercharged 9mm which would drive a plated bullet through body-armor. And an automatic pistol with a mushroom round that would stop a charging bull. She had never had to use anything but the pneumatic. She hoped she wouldn't have to now. And she was glad to have the Trooper on call. She thumbed her radio and called. "Jim, you hear me?"

"Katina, I hear."

"The boys have arrived. Three of 'em. If there's fun I'll tell you. So listen out."

"I will. Hope I can join the party."

"Only if you're invited!" She cut the radio, arranged her weapons, and cracked the window. Then she lay face down on the bed, watching and waiting.

As the night got darker the parties got louder. Laughter, shouts, songs, and squeals. More cars roared into the motel, pulling up outside rooms, welcomed by couples inside. Racing enthusiasts pouring in to party. By morning the only sober people in the Glen would be the drivers and their pit-crews. An orgy in the making. Katina was envious. She was lying alone on a bed watching the only silent room in the opposite block. Ruth Adams had brought her lover to the ideal place for a heist.

The row reached a crescendo around midnight, then quieted as the celebrants settled down to serious drinking and lovemaking. Yells from scattered fights and screams from possible rapes rolled across the parking lots. No police arrived. This must be a city-approved Saturnalia. The odd drunk staggered along the walkway opposite, trying various doors. The lovers' remained locked.

At around two the light went out in an alcove which held soft-drink machines and ice-cube dispensers. Katina slipped on night goggles, saw two shadows crouching beside the dark bulk of the machines. She raised the pneumatic rifle, rested the muzzle on the window ledge.

One shadow slipped up to the lovers' door and slapped something onto it. Plastic explosive! Blow the door, grab the woman, and get away while quieter neighbors were hoping the next rock wouldn't be through their windows.

Shouts and the sound of breaking glass were still coming from expiring parties.

Katina estimated the angle between alcove and door, aimed at the shadow in the alcove, fired, shifted to the shadow at the door. He started to run, then dropped. The one in the alcove had slumped at the base of the ice-cube dispenser.

She was already running across the lot. The driver of the Buick started to get out, saw her, and reached for his gun. A dart struck his stomach. He fell back behind the wheel. She pushed his legs in after him, slammed the car door, and went to the men on the ground.

The neighbors hadn't noticed or were being careful not to notice. Anyone who stumbled over the two unconscious bodies would think them two more drunks. She needed one for herself. She couldn't move either by herself. She unhooked the radio at her belt. "Jim? The party's halfway along the southeast wing. I've got three for you. Come fast if you want a slice of the action!"

"Four minutes!" He cut off.

Thank God for an intelligent and cooperative cop! She had parked her pneumatic behind the Coke machine and gone to drag the man away from the door when it opened and the woman she was protecting appeared. "What the hell's going on?"

"Don't know, ma'am." Katina straightened. "I'm a police officer. Special branch." She showed a badge. "Looks like this thug was doing a break-in on you." She gripped the man's hair and tilted his face to the light. "Know him?"

"Never seen him before in my life." Ruth Adams seemed more annoyed than alarmed. And why was she wearing a jumpsuit at two in the morning? Especially when Peter joined her wearing only a towel.

"Who's this? And what's this?" He touched the outside of the door. "Christ! Plastic! The bastard was going to blow the lock!" He glanced at the woman. "Pirenne?"

The flare of anger in her eyes told Katina that Pirenne was a name he should not have mentioned. "Peter—put some clothes on!" She turned to Katina. "What are you going to do with him?"

"There's a police cruiser coming. Both of you had best stay inside till I've cleared this muck from the door. No detonator in place so it's not really dangerous."

"Will you want a statement from us?"

"If you don't know who he is, there's not much you can say, is there, ma'am? I'm here because we were warned a gang from out of town might try something tonight." More shouts and more sounds of breaking glass. "They knew there'd be a lot of background noise!"

"Can we be of any help?"

"Thanks, but the cruiser's on its way. I may ask you for a statement later. Now, please go back to bed."

The woman smiled and closed the door. Katina wiped her forehead. Her hands were shaking. Alone with three paralyzed gunmen. Liable to be disciplined for exceeding or failing to fulfill her ambiguous orders. And all because she'd fallen in love with a bastard who thought he could handle a saber. It was his fault she was here. She'd only learned saber because of him. And the Service selectors had only picked her because she'd maneuvered the Intercollegiate Athletics Union into adding a female class to the saber division. They'd been more impressed by her winning it than by her Harvard law degree.

She resisted the impulse to kiss Jim when he arrived in his yellow and blue cruiser. As usual she overcompensated. "There's one in that car. Another in that alcove. And this specimen!" She pushed the body with her foot. "Cuff 'em while I get the antidote."

"Very good, ma'am." She saw his expression as he bent down to snap on the cuffs. What did he think so remarkable about one woman facing three gunmen? Why the hell did she have to act like some Amazon when she met an attractive man? She was still furious with herself when she returned from her room with the syringe, her anger made worse by knowing it was a reaction to terror.

"Useful stuff, that!" said Jim as she plucked the darts from the captives. "Wish we were allowed to use it."

"Nobody's allowed to use it! Unless you want to land me in the shit—forget I did." She slid the needle of the autoinject under the skin on the back of the first captive's hand. "It's dangerous. Occasionally stops 'em breathing before you can bring 'em round."

"So all we're allowed is a thirty-eight magnum that kills if it hits almost any place." He held up another cuffed hand for her to inject.

"I ignore idiot regulations. Usually I get away with it."

"I'll bet you do." He smiled as he hauled the first half-conscious prisoner to his feet. "Which of 'em do you want to talk to?"

"Talk to?" She glanced at him. A nice guy— but too quick on the uptake. More of her bad luck! She nodded at the man who had slapped on the plastic. "He'll do. Park him on the bed in Room 406, while I scrape off this goo. Put the others in your cruiser and wait with 'em."

"Whatever you say, ma'am." He pushed his

stumbling captive toward the entrance to her block.

She finished removing the plastic and walked toward her room, wondering if she could summon the guts to drag the truth out of her victim. She found him manacled on his back, staring at her with shark's eyes. A killer who would need persuading to talk, would stay silent to protect himself from his employer.

She stood, looking down at his face. She would have to lean hard to split this one. She loathed the prospect. Then she remembered the name Peter had gasped. The woman's angry reaction to its mention. "Pirenne sold you! That's why I was waiting."

An instant of confusion and hatred; then his face was again flat. But the flare was enough. She went into the bathroom, closed the door, and called Service Information on the extension, clipping on a scrambler while the computer reported the achievements of one of the world's most successful information brokers. By the time it had finished it would be morning in Paris. She got a Service tie-line and told the Paris operator to find LaCoste, a Greek-speaking Surite officer with whom she had worked and with whom she maintained a sentimental relationship.

"Pirenne?" he answered, speaking Greek to confuse tapes in Paris and Washington. "Yes—I know of him. Something about him in this morning's bulletin. Wait while I check. Yes— here it is. He's dead." And he told her how Pirenne had died.

She hung up, feeling sick, then went to the waiting cruiser. "Jim—collect that specimen on the bed. No, I haven't touched him. Didn't need to. Take 'em all to the station. Book 'em for attempted robbery, concealed weapons, illegal parking—anything you like, so long as you don't bring me into it. Credit's all yours."

She watched him go toward her room, then turned to the pair in the back of the cruiser. The same shark's eyes, the same transient shock when she named Pirenne. "Now he's dead. You'll get nothing from him. Not even revenge. And nothing except trouble from his killers. Some clients he'd conned. Unless you want them after you—better not croon his name. Or this job."

They stared back, cold and silent.

"Plead guilty, keep quiet, and take the rap!" Then to relieve her anger and add weight to her advice, she added, "If you drag me in, I'll make sure all three of you get life. I'm FBI!"

The name of the Agency impressed crooks as well as cops. The venom in her voice shattered their veneer. By the time Jim got back with the third they were promising not to cause her trouble.

The Trooper pushed the man into the back, then turned to her. "Anything else I can do for you, ma'am—Katina?" He had sensed there was.

The temptation to invite him back for breakfast or something after he had booked his prisoners was acute. But he was too damned smart to involve. "No time now. Maybe—if I'm through here again?"

A moment of mutual regret, then she watched the taillights of the cruiser disappear down the highway and went back to her room. She brushed out her hair with a furious energy, calmed her emotions, and phoned Ruth Adams.

"Officer Plastiras. In room 406. If you care to make a statement now I won't have to delay you in the morning."

"I'll be right over." Peter was protesting in the background. "The gentleman with me wants to come too."

"Good for him! But I'll take you first." She walked up and down the room as she waited, sharpening her mind for the coming battle of wits. A battle which, if lost, would bring wrath down on her from on high. A battle which, if refused, would block further promotion. Why the hell didn't the Service tell her what the real job was?

When Ruth Adams did arrive she was suddenly repelled by the prospect of playing cat and cat. She shut the door on Peter and turned to the woman. "Pirenne's dead!"

"Dead?" Just a shadow of shock.

"Killed yesterday in Paris. Customers he'd swindled. Caught him in his office. Shot him in the stomach. Drenched the room with gasoline. Fired it. He died of third-degree burns about six hours later. Six unpleasant hours. Know why?"

A trace of horror. "Should I?"

"Maybe! In his business the penalty for passing bogus is severe. And Mister Ward mentioned his name when he came to the door. That's why I checked on Pirenne. On what he does. And found he was murdered yesterday. Friend of yours?"

The woman shook her head. Her blue eyes hard, but dismay in them too.

"You one of his clients?"

"No."

"I can't make you talk. But you'd make it a lot easier for me if you'd say what all this is about." Katina let her anger gust. "Damnation! I've just saved you from having your door blown open. And from God knows what after that!"

"I owe you a lot. Those three—do they work for Pirenne?"

"Three? Only one at your door."

"I saw three put into the cruiser."

"Yes—three. Pirenne hired 'em. Professional

hit men. Were they after you or Mister Ward?"

"After me. Peter's not involved."

"After you for what?"

"Pirenne's an information broker. I guess you know that?"

Katina nodded. But how did this woman know about the seedy business of dealing in information. Information can't be traced like bank transfers or currency. In certain areas of business and politics it had become the preferred medium of exchange. "He was trying to buy from you?"

"He'd given up trying to buy. He'd started to squeeze. Some months ago three of his people attacked me. Peter was with me. We escaped. That's how Peter knows Pirenne's name. But he doesn't know anything else that's relevant."

This woman had been called a threat to both the UN and the US. She was being hunted by Quine. Hints that she was being hunted by other Agencies—domestic and foreign. The Service was interested in her—that's why Katina had been sent to join the hunt. And Pirenne had tried to grab her—twice! So she hadn't been an innocent open to attack. Pieces began to drop into place. She'd been dressed and ready. She'd laid a trail for the three in the Buick to follow. Looking into her face Katina wondered if the gunmen were lucky the police had them rather than this blue-eyed woman.

Better play the charade to the end. "What did he plan to squeeze out of you?"

"May I sit down?" The woman sank into a chair. "I was a diamond prospector on Nuerth."

"What?" The least likely role for this elegant woman.

"A successful one. I found a pipe and brought back a load. Worth more than I'll ever need. I sold through a reputable dealer in New York—Feinstein's on Forty-seventh Street. You can check with them. Ask about the "diamond girl'!"

"I hope I won't need to. How does Pirenne fit?"

Ruth Adams explained how he did. When she had finished Katina said, "So you told him. Why did he come at you again?"

The woman shrugged.

"Why was Pirenne murdered? He's no loss. Congratulations—if you were involved!"

"I was not!" The woman sprang to her feet, real fury on her face. Katina met it, blast for blast. And it was Ruth Adams who gave way. "Not directly. I had no idea anything so horrible—!" She sat down again. "But I am partly guilty."

"How? Did you feed Pirenne false information? Information he sold to somebody else, not knowing it was fake?"

"I didn't give him false information." The woman bit her lip; she was becoming more human as the enormity of what had happened sank in. "I gave him the coordinates of the pipe. The diamonds are there. Only—well, I didn't warn him about the quicksands."

"Quicksands? Nuerth quicksands?" Everybody had heard about those deadly sands. "So whoever bought from Pirenne assumed they'd been trapped. That Pirenne planned to resell the data after they'd been sucked down. That he didn't expect them to get back. So they squared accounts when some of 'em did! And he wouldn't even know why—not until he was afire!"

A broker's integrity must be unquestioned if he is to be successful. For an information broker dealing with information obtained by questionable means it is essential for his survival. The information he sells must be valid within the terms of the deal. The more dishonest he is in obtaining it, the more honest he must be with his customers. They cannot get recourse through the courts if they are swindled, so they may take it out on his person. Pirenne's customers evidently had.

"I only wanted to destroy the bastard's reputation. Not to get him killed—so horribly!

Nor to kill his customers. Those sands I didn't tell him about are shallow. Deep enough to scare—not deep enough to suffocate. Whoever bought from Pirenne must have known he'd played rough to get what he sold. So I played rough too."

"Some kind of a game?"

"I have a weakness—" She checked herself. "I swear I didn't think it would end in murder!" She paused. "What will you do?"

"Just check on your story. But I don't doubt it. Where are you heading?"

"To my house in Maryland. After I've taken Peter back to Ithaca." She looked at Katina. "I don't want him to know."

"Nothing I need to say to him. Don't even need to talk to him. This your address? I can talk to your lawyer? Your banker?' Katina paused. "The heat's off you, I should think. Pirenne's customers won't know where he got the data."

The woman stood up. "Then can I go now?"

Katina nodded. "Thank you for cooperating."

After Ruth Adams had gone Katina took another shower while she thought. The diamond story must be essentially true—too easy to check the facts, now she knew about Feinstein's and the "diamond girl." She already knew about the woman's wealth—about her place in Maryland.

The gunmen had been working for Pirenne. Their reactions to his name confirmed that. Doing what? Exacting revenge? But Pirenne could not have known he had retailed bogus until faced by his murderous customers. Only yesterday. And tonight's attempted grab had been a planned operation. The strike force had been in place watching Peter, waiting for him to lead them to the woman, when Pirenne was still ignorant of his doom. Had he known of his danger he wouldn't have been sitting in his Paris office waiting to be barbecued.

The contract had been for a living snatch. They had wanted a living woman. To tell something? More about diamonds? Hardly. For the same reason Bose and Sloan wanted her? More likely. Because other agencies wanted her? Most likely. Powerful people wanted to talk to her very much. Her picture had reached Unipol files. Which meant it had reached other agencies besides the FBI and her own. Foreign agencies. Her picture might have reached Pirenne. And he would have recognized his "diamond girl."

Information had been Pirenne's business. He collected it himself. Probably worked as a subcontractor collecting it for other people. Arranged jobs too dirty for respectable agencies to do. Information was like money. Clean so long as nobody knew how you'd got it.

No US agencies—not yet! But other governments, some multinationals, were less fastidious. Some countries no longer went to the danger and expense of maintaining large clandestine organizations of their own. Cheaper and safer to give a contract to a firm like Pirenne's.

When she had finished drying herself she went to the phone.

IX

"You spoke to her? But that was expressly forbidden. You saved her from kidnappers? She's safe and going to her home in Maryland?" Doctor Bose's voice echoed his confusion and disapproval. "You picked her up in Ithaca? She took him riding! On horses? Good God! What happened then?"

Sludic cut in on the extension. "Miss Plastiras, you will have to justify your actions. No—not by telephone. Come here. Trygvie Lie Towers. Doctor Bose's apartment. Today! No, I was not aware you were about to proceed on leave. Your leave is canceled. Report to us here, as ordered. What did you say? ... I thought you said that." He hung up and looked at Bose. "Alex, did you hear what Katina said?"

"Sada, she's done a good job. After all, if—"

"She's done an excellent job, even if she has exceeded her orders. And she has every right to curse me for stopping her vacation. However, such a remark directed at a senior is an unusual response for an Agent, is it not?"

"Katina's an unusual agent. She must have been shadowing Ward when the Adams woman picked him up. And took him riding. If she's not human how can she ride a horse?"

"The laws of physics are the same throughout the Arm. And riding animals are not peculiar to Earth."

"But a horse! Who'd have thought of that?"

"Only Alia apparently. Katina will give us the full story."

"Why the hell did you ask her to come here? This is a UN apartment. She'll realize immediately that one of us works for the United Nations."

"Alex, I'm quite sure that Katina has known that you work for the UN since the first day we met her. I'm reasonably sure she knows you're a Deputy Director-General."

"I hope she doesn't learn that my job is alien liaison. Because if she does, she'll probably tumble to what you are."

"That, I doubt. Katina is entirely human. I

have yet to meet a human who will accept the fact that a nonhuman like myself can mimic a human in both an external body and in social behavior. Humans have a mental block against accepting that any other race is capable of creating itself in the human God's image. You, Alex, are the exception that proves the rule. And had we not lived together, had you not seen my bathing upon occasion, I suspect even you would have rejected such a heretical idea."

"Damn you, Sada! You're getting too human to be comfortable." Bose paused. "Three thugs tried to kidnap Alia. Miss Plastiras saved her and had them arrested. Who employed them?" He looked at Sludic. "Did you expect something like that when you told Katina to protect Alia?"

"Suspect—not expect! I know there are others besides ourselves who would like to question Alia. I knew Unipol security would not keep our quest secret. There must now be several organizations who know a 'Galactic Marshal' is hunting an alien who looks like a woman. Alia is their target as well as ours."

"And you've let them? You left Katina by herself to protect Alia?"

"I did not think Katina would have to protect Alia. Alia has always been more than capable of protecting herself. I warned Katina of the danger of competing groups because I wanted her to be ready to protect herself if Alia was attacked." Sludic paused, thoughtful. "But Katina is a remarkable young lady. The more I learn about her the more remarkable I find her. On this occasion she probably pre-empted the kidnap attempt. But even had she not, I doubt it would have succeeded. We will learn what actually happened when she reports."

Katina hung up the phone and sat on the rumpled bed in her motel room staring at the instrument. Doctor Bose had reacted to her report as she had expected. Lester Sloan's refusal of her absurd request to quit the operation and go on vacation had also been appropriate. But the fact that he had not torn her to shreds when she had called him a bastard was out of character and left her feeling even more uneasy about this whole project. Every senior officer she knew would have started disciplinary action before she was off the phone. But this anonymous man from Washington had only seemed mildly surprised by her insult. There was something about Sloan which didn't ring true, and that something reminded her of something else. She sat, trying to remember what it was.

Presently she picked up the telephone again and asked Service Information for a report on

Doctor Alexander Selin Tanaka Bose and on Lester Sloan of Washington. The computer gave her the same answer it had given her three weeks earlier: Doctor Bose was a Deputy Director-General of the United Nations. There was no record of a Lester Sloan answering to her description of him anywhere in its data banks.

Katina hesitated, then decided to go for broke. She punched in a request coded with a key number she was not supposed to know, and which would probably get her suspended if the Service discovered she did. She again requested information about the pair, this time at the top security level.

The computer considered her new request, decided that as she had known the access coding to the top security data banks she must be authorized to access them (machine logic is strictly Aristotelian), and asked her to wait. She walked up and down the room while it searched, wondering why she was getting deeper and deeper into this mess, and trying to convince herself that it was the sort of thing the Service really expected her to do. Damn the Service! Why wouldn't it tell its officers what their real task was? She answered her own question as soon as she asked it. If you told agents what they were supposed to be doing that was all they did. If you gave them vague open-ended orders then you left them ready to notice anything, whether related to the ostensible object of an operation or not. Rational enough in the irrational world in which she lived, but tiring for the mind and bad for the nerves.

The telephone rang and she grabbed it, snapping on the scrambler. The computer was back with details of Bose's complete career. She listened, intrigued. Deputy Director-General with special responsibility for alien liaison. Alien liaison! Of course! That was the "something" about Sloan which had been nagging away at the back of her mind. She was not surprised when the computer continued to report that it had nothing, not even in its top secret files, about a Lester Sloan. It wouldn't have. Because Sloan was an alien. Probably a Galactic Marshal!

She forgot she was talking to a machine and thanked it for the information. Then she stood in the middle of the floor studying the reflection of her own naked body in the mirror while she considered what that information implied— alien involvement! Why had she not realized that before? She had heard about Galactic Marshals but had never met anybody who had seen one. She must have unconsciously suppressed the idea as being too bizarre; it was grotesque to imagine that any alien could mimic a human being well enough to pass as one. "Galactic Marshal" was just the exaggerated description used by a sensation-seeking journalist after encountering some alien hominoid.

But if such a creature as a Galactic Marshal existed, and if it could mimic a human being so well, then of course she would never know if she did see one, nor would anybody else. She had been suspicious of Sloan from the first; she had never suspected he might be an alien. But as soon as the computer had identified Bose as the UN's liaison with the aliens all sorts of slight inconsistencies in Sloan's speech and behavior began to fit into place.

Even more disquieting, what did that suggest about Ruth Adams? The woman had told the Athens Police that her age was twenty-eight and Katina, an expert at estimating the ages of men and women, would have accepted that age as correct, especially after seeing her tonight. Which would have made her a teenager when she went prospecting alone for diamonds on Nuerth.

But Ruth Adams was definitely a woman. After their confrontation Katina was certain of that. A woman being hunted by aliens and their human allies! In that kind of crunch Katina knew where her real duty lay. One of the Service's jobs was to protect humans against aliens. Whatever the transient difficulties offending the Auld might cause for the US or the UN, frustrating a Galactic Marshal's attempt to arrest a human woman served the long-range well-being of humanity. She had to keep her out of the alien's hands. Even if it wrecked her own career.

Katina sighed and began to dress. She was, in general, enjoying her life. She did not want to sacrifice herself for any cause, not even the cause of humanity in general. But the cause of a lone woman, harried by aliens, was a cause she could not betray. She must give Ruth Adams all the help she could. She rang her room a second time.

"I have some new and important information. Come over now—without Peter."

There was understandable caution in Ruth's voice. "Your room? No. Let's meet in the coffee shop. More public."

A strong-minded and sensible woman! Katina brushed her hair. Then she checked her automatic.

The two women studied each other across the table. At five in the morning the Coffee Shop was empty except for a few party-goers trying to recover. Katina's question was direct. "Miss Adams, are you human?"

"Am I human?" Controlled surprise. "Of course I am! Why ask?"

"Because I think you're being hunted by a Galactic Marshal."

"What?" Sudden tension, but not confusion.

"Have been hunted for weeks. Unipol had your picture and they matched it with one taken in the Athens airport. I'm attached to the FBI and got called in because I speak Greek. Another agent and I were sent to work with a Doctor Bose who pretends he's with Unipol. Actually he's the Deputy Director-General responsible for alien liaison. With him is a Lester Sloan who's supposed to be a mandarin in Washington. But he doesn't exist in even the top security records. I suspected he was a Galactic Marshal." She eyed Ruth steadily. "After seeing your reaction—I'm sure."

"And I," said Ruth, laughing, tension gone, sipping coffee, "thought I had only to look out for Pirenne's people. Now there's Unipol and an Auld Marshal after me. The FBI too?"

"My orders are to keep you under surveillance and protect you without your knowledge. That was what I was doing earlier tonight. When you came to the door—I lost my cover. Now you know me."

"Do I?" Ruth studied her. "Are you going to arrest me?"

"No. Nor are the others. Not arrest—they'll probably try a quick snatch. When nobody's watching. I think the Marshal plans to have

Unipol grab you after you've left Peter. But there are others who may not wait. Other agencies—not US. Foreign. International. You've got something they want. Something more than details about diamonds."

"This Galactic Marshal—does he know where I am now?"

"He knows where you were. I spoke to Bose on the phone after the incident. To report. That's when I caught on to this Sloan being a Marshal. And not too bright! He hung up without asking me where we were. I told him you were heading for Maryland."

"Why are you telling me all this?"

"Because I believe you're human. An unusual human who goes prospecting for diamonds, alone, at seventeen! But a human just the same. And any woman being hunted by an alien has my sympathy."

"Thank you, Katina." She paused. "You may be just the kind of person I've been looking for. Where's this Galactic Marshal now?"

"With Bose in New York. I've been ordered to report to his apartment today."

"I must meet him. I'll go with you.'

"What?" Katina stared. "After I've warned you? He'll grab you. And if he gets you to a Terminal he can do what he likes with you. The Terminals are Auld territory. Nobody'll try to stop him from taking you there. No politician is going to risk a power cutback just to rescue one woman. You know how those damned Auld start to squeeze if we don't dance to their tune. They've been squeezing already. That Doctor Bose—he's a decent man at heart. He hates this business. The Marshal's conned him into it, probably by claiming you're an alien mimic. I don't think Bose believes that anymore." She paused, then shrugged. "Anyway how can any human stop an Auld with a side-arm from doing what he likes?"

"I can, Katina. Thanks for the warnings but I must meet the Marshal—and soon. I'll get his promise of a safe-conduct first, of course."

"You'll trust your life to an alien's word?"

"I'd trust any Auld's word before I'd trust most human oaths. The Auld have their faults, but lying isn't among them."

"You must know a hell of a lot about them to say that."

"I do. That's why they're hunting me."

"And that's why there're other gangs trying to grab you? Maybe they're more dangerous than the Auld. They suspect you're an alien, or you know a lot about aliens. Either way that will let them use any brutality needed to make you talk. There are lots of otherwise decent people who'll be ready to toss you into any kind of hell for the good of all. If you know something that will help Earth to put one over on the Auld, and you refuse to share it with the rest of us, then any tool that can dig it out of you is ethical!" Katina leaned forward and gripped Ruth's hand. "I may not know much about the Auld but I know a hell of a lot about my colleagues. And they're pussycats compared to some other organizations, domestic and foreign! Drop the whole business and go for cover. I know places where neither Auld nor humans will ever catch you."

"Thanks again!" Ruth stood up. "What's the Marshal's phone number?"

"Christ—you can't phone him! They can trace a call in seconds these days."

"Not the way I key a call." There was a half-smile on her lips, as though she was relishing the prospect of danger. She took a dollar coin from her pocket and went to the pay phone on the wall. "Katina—the number!"

She knew she shouldn't give it, but when she had touched Ruth's hand a contact seemed to have closed, binding the two of them in trust. She gave the number, watched Ruth drop in the dollar, recover the coin, and start keying. The process went on for some time and Katina began to appreciate the range and variety of long-distance code routings this woman must know.

Ruth caught her eye, smiled, and covered the mouthpiece. "It's ringing now. They'll trace the call back to the bar on Nuerth. A bar with a clientele that doesn't like snoopers!" Her smile was so infectious that Katina found herself smiling back. Then her morale sagged. She had nothing to smile about. By giving Ruth the number she had probably finished her career in the Service and perhaps directed Ruth into a trap. As was her habit in moments of despondency she cursed the swordsman whose ineptitude with a saber was the initial cause of the present debacle.

Ruth was speaking. "May I talk to Mister Sloan, please?" . . . "Yes, I know it's five in the morning." . . . "I'd rather tell him who's calling myself." . . . "Sada! Is that you?" The expression of delight which crosses a child's face when some adult is caught by the child's joke passed across hers. "Can't you guess?" . . . "Yes, Alia, of course."

She stood listening for a few moments and then spoke with a hint of sharpness. "That was not my fault, and you know it!" . . . "In any case, that's long past. I've called you out of bed to ask for a meeting. Under safe-conduct, of course." . . . "Twenty-four hours at least." . . . "Sada, it would take you twenty-four hours to trace this call, so don't procrastinate!"

She listened, then cut in sharply, "Now I know you're on Earth. I won't give you a second chance to meet me unless you agree to meet me today." ... "Within the next twelve hours. I'll come to Doctor Bose's apartment before noon today." ... "Yes, I understand. Your command of colloquial English is excellent." ... "Miss Plastiras? She's with me. I'll bring her to our meeting. She gave me your number and location. Also certain other details." ... "Of course she's unharmed! Sada, I resent that! You know I prefer gentle methods for gaining cooperation. Not like some of the thugs you seem to be employing!" ... "Don't let's argue about that now. And you know that Miss Plastiras is not to be blamed in any way for my being able to get in touch with you. She's done us both a service, and I'm binding you to keep her role in our meeting confidential." ... "Before noon then ..." "Wait in your suite. And Doctor Bose must be present." ... "Sada, I insist! No Bose, no meeting!" ... "I'm glad you don't understand." ... "See you later today. Now go back to sleep!" She laughed and hung up. "It's all set. The Marshal—his name's Sada Sludic, by the way—thinks you're my prisoner. Sludic's an Auld and can't lie. I'm a human, and I lie with imagination and skill!" She sat down and finished her coffee. "I've promised to surrender you to him when we start our meeting."

"You told that alien you'd captured me?"

Katina could not keep her fury from her face. "My reputation in the Service—"

"Will remain untarnished!" Ruth leaned across the table and took the angry agent's hand. "Only four of us will ever know about this charade. Sludic, Bose, you, and I. And none of us will ever speak of it without your leave."

Katina knew it was irrational but she was soothed by Ruth's touch. "When are you going to meet the Marshal?"

"He assumed I'd be there at noon. So we'll arrive on his doorstep as soon as we can get to New York." She stood up. "Now I must make my farewells to Peter. I'll leave him my car. We'll drive to New York in yours." She smiled and left.

She was not smiling when she returned. Her expression was so grim that Katina hardly spoke until they were out on the highway, heading into the dawn. Then she said, "Please keep a look out astern. In case some other gang has picked up your trail and tries to jump us."

"I hope they do! I'd enjoy a fight right now!" Ruth sat silent for a while, then said, "Unless they've got a bug on us, we're clear."

"I looked for bugs while you were saying good-bye to Peter." Katina hesitated, then confessed. "I had a bug on him."

"You did?" Ruth glanced at her, seemingly

more pleased than annoyed. "I checked but didn't find yours. That reinforces what I said earlier. You may be the kind of person I've been looking for."

"To do what?"

"Help me get what I'm after."

"Tell me who you are first!"

"I'm Ruth Thalia Adams. My enemies call me Alia and my friends—if I had any—would call me Thalia."

"That's what Peter Ward called you? Isn't he your friend?"

"Peter's my lover." Thalia's lips tightened. "Or was."

"Was? You're dumping him?"

"I'm turning him loose. I don't want to. He's a delightful lover, a good poet, and a decent man. But I've got him involved with my own troubles already. I like him too much to lead him any deeper." She bit her lip. "People who get involved with me get into trouble. You're finding that out. I've fouled your operation up already."

"I'm used to having my operations go wrong in the middle. They usually straighten out before the end." The sun came up, blinding, as they crested a hill and Katina turned down the sun visor. "You haven't told me what yours is yet."

"It's dangerous to know what I'm up to."

Thalia glanced at her. "And you're dangerous to drive with."

"Never racked one up yet!" But Katina took the next series of bends less like a Watkins Glen enthusiast. "If you want me to help you, tell me what you're doing. Who you are."

"You're standing into danger!"

"Listen!" said Katina in sudden exasperation. "What's more dangerous than what I'm doing now? And danger's my thing—God knows why! Masochism—or a death-wish—or something! Should have gone in for mountain climbing or auto racing! They're safer than what I do for a living."

"Katina—we'd make a good team." Thalia was emerging from the depression of leaving her lover.

"A team to do what? Tell me who you are— then we'll talk about teams."

"Who I am—later perhaps. Will you settle for knowing what I'm after? And what I'd like you to do?" They whipped round a curve— Katina's Ford was only externally battered. Internally it was among the fastest on the road. "At present, I want you to drive slower."

"Sorry!" Katina eased back. "Okay! I'll buy. What are you trying to do?"

"Rescue the Auld from their own folly. And the human race from theirs. No—I'm not a crazy egoist. I can only start things moving.

But I've got to start somewhere, and that seems to be here." Thalia paused. "I'll need help. Want to learn more? If you do, you'll be involved. Whether you like it or not."

"That's what they said to me when I asked about the Service. If they answered, I'd be hooked. And I was!" Her hands tightened on the wheel. "I'm so damned inquisitive it'll kill me! Okay—I'm hooked again. How can I help?"

Thalia told her as they went up the cloverleaf onto the New York Thruway.

X

Sludic and Bose were eating breakfast when the security guard called from the lobby. "Two ladies here, sir. Insist they've got an appointment with the Doctor." The camera panned and Bose found himself looking into the brown eyes of Katina Plastiras and the blue eyes of the woman with her. He stared and, although neither could see him, pulled his robe closed.

"Shall I ask them to wait, sir?" prompted the guard.

"Yes—no! Send them up." His caution was swamped by the sight of Katina safe.

"Who is it?" Sludic looked up from the table, saw the two faces a moment before they disappeared from the screen, and jumped to his feet. "That's Alia! Stop them, Alex!"

"I can't! They're on their way up."

Sludic cursed in Auld. "She said she'd arrive at noon! A lie to catch me off guard!"

"She said she'd be here by noon. That means before noon. And nine's before noon." Bose hurried toward his bedroom. "I must get dressed."

"No!" Sludic caught him at the door. "It is I who must get dressed. Miss Plastiras must not see me like this." For the Marshal, clothes did indeed make the man, more than ever after a few hours' sleep. Left to itself the Auld body tended to make minor adjustments to gravity and posture. The Marshal disappeared into his suite, leaving Bose to meet Alia and her hostage.

When the chimes sounded and he opened the door, Katina did not look or act like a hostage. "Good morning, Doctor." She stepped past him into the hall. "Where's Mister Lester Sloan?"

"Dressing. Er—we weren't expecting you so early. We—!" He stood in gaping silence as the second woman came through the door, tried to protest when she followed Katina into the lounge. A woman whose beauty only a man could appreciate. The perfect features of the Athenian goddess. The Lady of the Bright Eyes!

The eyes were laughing. "I'm Ruth Adams.

Also known as Alia. You must be Doctor Bose?"
She held out her hand.

He had taken it before he realized that this
was no way to greet a Galactic fugitive. He
continued to hold it because a warmth flowed
from her grip. A comfort he had not felt since
his mother—

Alia retrieved her hand and looked around.
"So Sludic's restoring himself, is he?"

"Mister Sloan's dressing." Bose wished he
could do the same. He was not usually over-
concerned with his appearance, but at that
moment he was acutely conscious of his un-
shaved chin, of his paunch, of his balding head,
of his general lack of beauty. He gestured the
women toward chairs. "Please sit down. Would
you care for some coffee?" This was their
quarry. Very dangerous if cornered, Sludic had
said! And he was offering her coffee! But he
couldn't think of anything better to say.

"We've been drinking coffee all night. If we
drink any more we'll be awake for a week. But
thank you for asking." Alia relaxed into Sludic's
chair. "How long for him to pull himself
together?"

"A few minutes. Perhaps—" How much did
this woman know? And how much had she
told Katina? The hostage was watching her
captor with more amusement than alarm.

"At present he probably looks like a lump of

Silly Putty that's been left to stand!" Alia laughed, a musical laugh.

"I don't—" He glanced at Katina.

"I know that Mister Sloan is a Galactic Marshal," said Katina. "And that you're the Deputy Director General of the United Nations responsible for alien liaison."

"She also knows about shape-shifting," added Alia. "And you know what a mature Auld looks like, don't you, Doctor?"

He clutched his robe closer. "There are certain anatomical differences. But I cannot—"

Alia stood up. "As a physician you are familiar with human anatomy, both male and female, aren't you?" She started to unzip her jumpsuit.

"Of course. No—please, Miss Adams! Not here!" For Alia, having unzippered her suit, stepped out of it, and started to loosen her brassiere.

"Why not? Katina's a woman like me. And you must have seen thousands of naked women in your time. So I want you to see that I'm one. Before Sludic arrives. Not that I have anything that could possibly interest him." She dropped her panties and stood naked in the sunlight from the penthouse windows.

Bose tried to speak and choked; silenced by the beauty before him. The white skin, the smooth shoulders, the glowing hair falling about them, firm breasts, flat belly, slim thighs—

She smiled at his expression, put her arms high above her head, and turned slowly, offering him her every aspect. A woman relishing her own loveliness as only a lovely woman can. Men desire women, but women desire to be desired. No shape-shifter could possibly mimic that body, nor that feminine half-smile. The smile that showed her pleasure at his frank admiration.

She dropped her arms and turned to face him. "Doctor Bose, after seeing me naked, can you believe the absurdity that I'm not human?"

"No," said Bose quickly. "No indeed! You're the most beautiful woman I've ever seen."

"And you, Katina. What do you think?"

"Most of you's pretty good. Your breasts are on the small side. Of course, some men—"

"Alia—stop that nonsense!" Sludic was standing in the doorway, shrugging his shoulders as he made final adjustments to his torso but already the model of a tall human male.

"Good morning, Sada Sludic." Alia bent gracefully to pick up her underwear, stepping into her panties, snapping on her brassiere, zipping up her blue jumpsuit. Then she shook out her hair and turned toward him, smiling. "I've just been convincing the Doctor that I'm what I claim to be."

"What you are is immaterial!" Sludic advanced into the room. "What is material is the order for your arrest for a variety of offenses, committed all over the Transit System. I have come to Earth to collect you and put you where you can do no harm."

"And I came here in the hope that we can resolve our differences. That we can reach an agreement that would let me live in peace without being harried at intervals by your obsessive-compulsive single-minded gang of Transit Guards. That would let you concentrate on your duties as a Senior Commissioner. Do you realize that deserting your Commission at intervals to chase after me is hastening the decay of the Authority it is your duty to preserve? And that your efforts are useless, for you will never catch me?"

"Alia, I have caught you! At least, I will catch you as soon as this silly safe-conduct is over. If you are wise you will surrender to me now. You are being hunted by humans far more ruthless than I."

"Somebody's called out the hounds! Was it you, Sada?"

"Of course not! I instructed both the Director-General and the Director of Unipol to maintain strict secrecy. My orders have been ignored. Half the clandestine agencies on Earth are hoping to seize you for their own stupid ends. As soon as I have put you somewhere safe I will teach these people not to disobey a Commissioner's order."

"As you're the first Commissioner ever to have visited this backwater planet, the locals have never had the chance of disobeying one before. Thank God they did! If they'd acted like the gutless wonders who run most worlds, I'd have been ashamed to call myself human!"

"This is a pointless discussion." Sludic cracked his knuckles. "You asked for this meeting to beg for a truce—"

"Sada Sludic, I haven't begged for anything since I was a child."

"I cannot grant you a truce. I cannot make peace with law-breakers. I can promise that, if you surrender, you will be allowed to live in peace on a peaceful world."

"Exiled to Larga? Dumped among a bunch of scholars to die of boredom!"

"Alia, you could do worse than modulate your ingenuity with some wisdom!"

"I'm asking you to leave me alone. Now that I'm home at last."

"Home? You never claimed Earth as home."

"When we first met 'Earth' meant nothing to you. Now, it means too much."

"Too much? What devious nonsense are you attempting now?"

"You Auld were high-tech barbarians when you learned how to drive Transits. You didn't drive them to spread civilization—not at first! You went out to loot! Perhaps the arrival of humans revived that memory in your Directors? Perhaps that's why they're keeping Earth a closed planet. Afraid of what you once were? Afraid that—"

"Enough!" Sludic's voice was a blow that stopped even Alia in full flight. "There may be some truth in that. But the present truth is that this time tomorrow you will be either dead or under arrest."

"Arrest for what?" She turned to Bose. "What crime have I committed on Earth that deserves arrest? Obtaining an obsolete passport? Defending myself against kidnappers? And against young men who pinch my bottom?"

"No crime, Madam!" Bose, suddenly resolute and determined, turned to face the Marshal. "This woman is human and so outside your jurisdiction."

Sludic sighed. "Alia, you are bringing disaster down on Alex and Katina. On many other humans also. You are too dangerous to roam free. Unless you surrender I will squeeze until the UN delivers you to me. Dead or alive! Earth's halfway to a hydrogen economy. I have only to reduce the supply of electrical power for electrolysis—"

"You'd punish a guiltless world just to catch me?"

"Earth is hardly guiltless! You know that."

"Nor are you Auld guiltless." She studied his face. "If ever there's a guilt-racked race, it's yours, Sada! You've appropriated more guilt for yourselves than you've earned!" She laughed. "So why not add some of your own, my Marshal? Why not break your oath of safe-conduct and execute me here and now? That would solve your problem, and save Earth from having to accept part of the guilt for my capture!"

"You know I cannot break an oath." The Marshal gave a gesture of disgust. "And execution is an admission of defeat. A defeat for both of us. I only want to take you to be questioned by the Directors—"

"By Christ!" said Bose, reverting to his maternal grandfather's religion, "You'll not take any woman off-world to be tortured! Not if you close up every damned Transit—"

"Not tortured, Alex! Questioned. We have no need of torture. That's a human specialty."

"I'll not arrest her!"

"Alia!" Sludic's voice was a plea. "Can't you see what you're doing?"

"If you leave me alone I swear to remain on Earth. And I swear to remain silent about everything off-world."

"I'm beginning to believe you may be human. Yet I'd accept your word, if that was all there was to it. But other humans won't let you stay silent. Too many already suspect you've tricked the Transits. Some know you have. They'd persuade themselves that extreme interrogation was justified to force secrets from you that might help Earth to throw off 'alien tyranny.' Katina's partner, Quine, does not yet suspect what you are, but he's hungry to get his hands on you. He promised that when he did he'd have you confessing to anything within twenty-four hours."

"Gerald Quine is an exaggerating bastard!" snapped Katina.

"There are others who can do what he claims he can. Even you might not be able to endure their methods. I have no option. I must take you with me. If you stay on Earth I can only let you stay here dead." Sludic paused. "If you surrender to me I promise Peter Ward will not be harmed."

"Peter! You dare to threaten Peter?" Alia was halfway across the room before Bose or Katina could move. But Sludic had moved. His hand had gone to his pocket as hers had gone to her belt-pouch. They halted, almost toe-to-toe. When Bose and Katina jumped toward them Alia hissed, "Back! Back—both of you! Or we're all liable to be disintegrated!"

The tableau held for almost half a minute. Then Sludic spoke softly. "Alia, can you see the danger you carry with you? How rousing your emotions takes you to the verge of spreading destruction?"

"You shouldn't have threatened Peter." Alia slowly relaxed and moved her hand from her waist. "Sada—I've misjudged you! I always knew that your damned sense of duty could force you into pressuring a population. I never imagined you capable of punishing an innocent individual. And Peter is innocent. All he knows about me is that I made a fortune in Nuerth diamonds."

"I would deeply regret having to take action against Peter Ward. He is a young poet of great promise, already achieving fame everywhere except on Earth. But you are his friend and so pressure on him is pressure on you. I must use whatever means are necessary—"

"Sada—you're infected! You've acquired the worst human attitudes along with your imitation human good looks!"

"I admit that. And I regret it." Sludic paused, his features too hard to be human. "I will do whatever I must to persuade you to surrender before other innocents die. And you know me well enough to know that I mean what I say."

"I'm learning that you can be as brutal an animal as anybody on Earth—or off it!" Alia bit her lip, then laughed. "Take Peter then, if you want him. I've finished with him. If you make him suffer to no effect, then you'll suffer for it. You'll punish yourself for your own injustice. You have both the cruelty and the conscience of the true zealot. Well, I'm no zealot! Nor am I a sentimental fool. You won't bring me to heel by threatening to whip Peter!"

"Alia, I cannot read minds but I can read emotions. You are lying! You will not sacrifice your friend to save yourself. Especially when your own life is not endangered, but only your freedom to make mischief."

"Miss Adams," Bose interrupted. "As a human you are protected by Treaty—"

She silenced him with a wave. "Sludic, if I surrender, will you swear that Peter will not be harmed? Nor will these two?"

"I swear they'll not be harmed by me. I swear I'll protect Peter. Alex also. He is my friend. I would like Katina to be my friend."

Bose opened his mouth to deny any such friendship, then closed it again. Alia had been bluffing and Sludic had called her bluff. Her instinctive reaction to the Marshal's threat, the pain on her face, denied her words. She had recognized the Auld fixity of purpose and she would not sacrifice her lover to save herself. And, despite himself, Bose felt a measure of sympathy for Sludic. A sympathy that stopped him denying friendship.

"Doctor Bose, Katina," Alia was saying. "Thanks for trying to help me. You've no responsibility for what happens now. You will not have to arrest me. Once I have settled my affairs I will go with Sada to the nearest Terminal and surrender on Transit territory. Is that agreeable, Sada?"

"Your affairs here—how long will that take?"

"The time to telephone my lawyer and have him transfer most of my property to Peter. So he can live as a poet and remember me as a man. I must sign a power of attorney, so someone can settle my few accounts. I must pay wages in lieu of notice to my housekeeper and gardener."

"I'm a lawyer," said Katina. "If I can help—?"

"A lawyer also! Then I will name you my executor. No—an exectuor is for wills, isn't it? And you can't make a will to take effect before you're dead, can you? So I'll give you my power of attorney. Will you arrange the details with my lawyer when I've told him what I want?" She looked at Sludic and laughed. "Why so morose in victory, Sada? Do you also see the boredom ahead now you have cornered me at last?"

"I am in no danger of being bored until you are safely on Larga."

"May I phone my lawyer and write a note to Peter?" She saw the doubt on Sludic's face. "You can listen to my conversation and read the letter."

The Marshal gestured and she went to the phone.

They listened to her instruct an evidently protesting lawyer on how she was proposing to dispose of her wealth. "I'm retiring to a kind of convent, Julian. I have to get rid of all my worldly goods before they'll let me in. Miss Katina Plastiras will have my power of attorney. Yes—she graduated from Harvard Law School. That's good, isn't it? Call back in fifteen minutes with the draft and she'll speak to you." She hung up the phone. "That's the time he needs to draw up such a crazy document. He wanted a couple of months, but settled for a quarter of an hour!" She turned to Sludic. "Let me relieve you of some anxiety, Sada." She took a small blaster from her belt-pouch and handed it to him in the traditional gesture of surrender. Bose felt sick as he thought of the moment when two blasters might have gone off simultaneously in the middle of the room. They'd have taken out the Tower and the UN!

Sludic accepted the weapon with a slight bow and his relief showed he too had been considering the worst-case outcome.

Alia went to the desk. "Now I must write a good-bye note to poor Peter. Better not use UN letterhead, eh, Doctor Bose?"

He found her some plain paper, then escaped to shave and dress. The sudden ending to the hunt left him feeling sad and empty. When he was dressed he returned to the lounge and stood watching Alia as she bent over the desk, writing her farewell letter to Peter Ward. His heart ached to think that such beauty was to disappear from Earth, to be wasted on the air of some alien world. But among the four of them she was now the most lighthearted. She's like some girl going off on a vacation, he thought, almost resentful that she should treat her own tragedy so lightly. And vaguely suspicious that she had surrendered so easily.

The phone rang. Her lawyer had evidently learned to live up to his promises when dealing with Alia. Katina started a legal discussion. Sludic stood fidgeting—the Marshal was acquiring more human habits every day. Alia finished her letter and handed it to him to read, together with a copy. "The copy's for Katina," she said.

Sludic read them both, nodded, and handed them back. "He will always be your friend!"

Katina hung up the phone. "He's a good lawyer. He'll do as he's told. And I'll keep an eye on Peter." She began to organize the scribbled draft she had copied down. "This is rough but legal. Sign here, Alia. Now you, Doctor. I need two witnesses, so I'll need yours as well, Marshal. I guess you'd better sign as Lester

Sloan. That's your Earthly alias, isn't it?" Katina too seemed remarkably composed.

Alia laughed as the Marshal signed. "Another first for me! First human to have an Auld witness a power of attorney." She folded her letter to Peter and put it in an envelope. "There's a mailbox in the lobby downstairs. I have the greatest faith in the US mails." She stood up and looked around the apartment. "You picked comfortable quarters, Sada. Will you let me have a cell as comfortable?"

"We do not have cells. Those are—"

"Another unattractive human custom?" She turned to Katina, the prisoner was in command. "Will you drive all four of us to the New Jersey Transit Terminal in your unique Ford?"

"She's talking as if she were going to catch a plane for Athens rather than a Transit to God knows where!" Bose followed the other three from the apartment, wild ideas of rescue rising in his mind. Katina must have sensed what he was thinking for she tugged him aside while they waited for the elevator. "Don't try!" she whispered. "Leave it to Thalia. She's got something more powerful than any blaster. Herself!"

XI

An endless stream of traffic poured along the thruway; the roads serving the Transit Terminals were now the busiest highways on Earth. Electrical distribution towers marched like giants across the countryside; the Terminals were Earth's main energy source as they were the source of energy for all the worlds in the system. All roads lead to the Auld, Bose thought, all power radiates from them. Ahead, on a low hill, the New Jersey Terminal was a gateway to the Spiral Arm. For Alia, sitting with Sludic in the rear of the Ford, it was the door to a prison.

Trucks were peeling off to pass through the gates in the perimeter fence, rolling down the slope to the bays, unloading shipments of other worlds, collecting cargoes from all over the system. A kilometer farther and buses were turning into the passenger terminal where humans would catch the Transit to Nuerth and aliens could leave for wherever in the system they wanted to go.

"Straight on," said Sludic, and his voice, his reflection in the rear-view mirror, showed his tension. Bose caught Alia's eye and her quiet smile wrenched his heart.

The next turn-off wound up the hill toward a complex of single-story buildings. They were entering Transit territory: the area no human was allowed to enter. Ahead were twin barriers: a visible fence and an invisible field.

"Keep going, Katina." Sludic leaned forward. "They're expecting us."

As if on cue the gate swung upward and the field must have opened, for Bose did not feel the tingle warning an intruder that if he pushed farther he would be knocked out. As the gate closed behind the car he felt the same bitter resentment some of his ancestors had felt when they found themselves fenced out of a part of their own country.

Katina, at Sludic's direction, stopped the Ford outside the main entrance to the buildings. Bose stared around, trying to absorb all he could while he had the chance. But the parking-lot, the cars, the red-brick buildings were more like the civic center in a small American town than offices of the Authority which ran the Transits and controlled the worlds they connected.

Sludic jumped from the car, called "Wait here!" and disappeared into the building.

Bose turned around in his seat and looked Alia full in the face. "Who are you?"

"Who am I? I hardly know myself."

"How can we help you?" asked Katina from beside him.

"You have already helped me far more than I had any right to expect. I never imagined I would hear an Auld of Sada's seniority asking two humans to be his friends. You may have saved my life already. You've humanized the Marshal. When he first arrived on Earth he must have been so angry and frustrated that if he'd caught me, he'd have shot me the moment he got me onto Transit territory. He'd have suffered agonies of guilt for it afterwards, but that wouldn't have helped me. Now you've got him feeling guilty before he's done anything!"

"Is he—will he—?"

"He'll keep his word. That's a major Auld weakness that can be properly exploited. As you may have learned. My interrogation will be mild. Then they'll exile me to Larga, where I shall spend my days absorbing wisdom. And also learning a hell of a lot more about the Transit Authority." She laughed and squeezed Bose's shoulder. "Don't shed any tears over my fate. If I don't manage to dodge it, then I'll deserve it!"

"Is there nothing we can do?" asked Katina.

"There is. But I'm not sure you can do it."

"I can try!"

"Then accept the friendship that Sludic's offering. You may never understand how hard it is for him to offer friendship to an alien—I mean, to people he regards as alien. Nor how much he needs friendship. He is quite alone now, and loneliness for an Auld is the nearest thing to hell. It won't make him swerve one iota from what he decides is his duty. But it may make him modify his decisions about what his duty is."

"What kind of friendship—?"

"Human friendship. It's hard, after all this, isn't it? But having a Marshal as a friend is the most powerful weapon you can give Earth. And don't underestimate him. He can be ruthless where duty's concerned."

"Where are you from?" Bose made a last desperate effort to solve the enigma of this beautiful and infuriating woman.

"From all over!" She leaned forward and kissed him. Then she kissed Katina. "There's Sada now. I must go. It's unwise and impolite to keep a Marshal waiting!" She laughed, got out of the car and without looking back walked to where Sludic was standing at the bottom of the steps.

Bose watched her, a lump in his throat, her kiss hot on his lips. He heard her speaking clearly, loud enough for both of them to be sure of her words. "I freely surrender to the Transit Authority!"

Sludic nodded and waved his hand. Eight Guards in combat gear, their visors closed, came from the building and surrounded her. Sludic stepped aside and she started to walk up the steps, the squad moving with her. Every one of them carried a side-arm capable of destroying cities, yet they treated her with an obvious wariness and she was escorted rather than led into the building.

"That's no way to secure a prisoner," muttered Katina with professional disapproval.

Sludic waited until Alia and her escort had disappeared then came over to the car. He got into the rear seat. "Back to New York."

Bose stared at him. "You mean—you're going to leave her here?"

"She'll be quite safe—and comfortable. I have to close down my operation before I can take her to Gadon." When Bose still hesitated, he snapped, "Alia'll be all right. In fact she's already amusing herself by confusing her escort.

You never realized she speaks Galact, did you? Well—she does! Now, for God's sake, let's get out of here." When they had rejoined the traffic streaming away from the Terminals, he added, ":She speaks Auld too."

"I thought—"

"You thought that nobody but an Auld speaks Auld? So did I. Until I met Alia. She not only speaks it, she speaks it fluently. But she's damned careful nobody catches her doing it." Sludic stretched his legs as well as he could in the car. "Now can you see why she's dangerous?"

"Dangerous to you perhaps. She'd be of great help to us."

"Help? She'd have you quarreling with half the Arm if she told your politicians all she knows. I'll give her credit—she never let out a hint of anything off-world while she was on Earth."

Bose felt too dispirited to argue. "Are we going back to my apartment?"

"Yes." Sludic paused. "There's nowhere else I can go."

Katina broke in. "We'll have to stop for fuel. And I need food. Also a washroom. There's a service area five kilometers ahead."

"Then go there! But don't leave by the fire exit or use the phone until we've discussed your future."

They walked together into the service center, went their separate ways, and met again at a table in the restaurant. Katina had a loaded plate. Sludic brought two coffees, one for himself and one for Bose. They sipped their coffee and watched Katina eat.

Presently Sludic said, "Katina, you are Alia's agent."

"I'm her attorney. If my chiefs allow it."

"They will. I'll make sure the Service sends you on extended leave."

"The Service? What Service?" asked Bose.

"She'd rather not mention who she works for." Sludic was now relaxed and seemed to enjoy baiting the angry-eyed young woman on the other side of the table.

"What makes you think that my chiefs will take orders from you?"

"The orders won't come from me. They'll come from your President. Who will get them from the Director-General. Properly disguised of course." Sludic leaned forward. "Did you imagine I'd allow anybody to help me in the hunt for Alia without knowing everything about him—or her? I'll arrange for you to be free to do what you promised Alia you would. Your first task will be to inform Professor Ward that Miss Adams has transferred most of her property to him."

"I'll be telling him that, whatever orders I get."

"I advise you not to tell him anything else. In her letter she didn't say who she is or where she's gone. So she doesn't want him to know. If you tell him it will only increase his unhappiness."

"I don't know who she is, so I can't tell Peter or anybody else. And I've got a copy of her letter. She's let him assume she's gone to Nuerth and won't be back. He can go on thinking that. For all I know it's the truth."

"She's not coming back. That much is certain." Sludic eyed Katina. "Have you ever considered working for the Transit Authority?"

"Work for you Auld? Of course not! Has any human ever been asked?"

"Not yet. Six weeks ago such an invitation would have been as unthinkable to me as it is to you. But after six weeks on this world, after living with you humans, after our operation, I can see that, sooner or later, we'll have to invite you to take your share of the transit load."

"Why?" asked Bose, not expecting an answer.

But Sludic was acting less and less like an Auld and he did answer. "Because, Alex, you humans have just that combination of energy, ethics, and malice the job needs. We have carried the burden for too long." He looked away, across the half-empty restaurant. "It'll be generations before you're ready to take real responsibilities, but we have to start some time. And preferably with people like Katina and youself." He swung round to face them. "Katina, don't reject any invitation out of hand. Wait until you've consulted your superiors. I suspect they'll jump at the chance of planting one of their people in the Transit Administration."

Bose was still trying to digest Sludic's offer when Katina asked, "Marshal, do you know the main reason I'd be chary of working for the Authority?"

"A distaste for being regarded as a traitor to your race?"

"That would be the least of my reasons. The chief one is because I'm not sure I'd want to get mixed up with an organization which is basically so incompetent. Hunting one woman across the Arm—and then needing human help to catch her!"

Sludic's face ceased to look human and showed the alien anger beneath. Bose caught his breath and Katina made a small instinctive escape movement. Then the human mask returned, but the voice was still icy. "So you have already noted one of our many weaknesses! That makes me all the more anxious to have you working for the Authority. I will make you a written offer after I am back in New York.

You can show that offer to your seniors and be guided by their orders."

Katina relaxed and shrugged. "I'll have to report anyway. What should I tell them—from your point of view?"

"Tell them the truth. They already know that I'm a Marshal. Show them my offer. They'll urge you to take it. Tell them I'll be ordering you to open a law office in Washington—to act as an unregistered disguised lobbyist for the Transit Authority. They'll understand that. You'll be able to do all the spying you want. Your only immediate job will be to act as Alia's lawyer."

"Sludic!" Bose burst out. "You can't involve the girl—"

"I'm no girl!" She studied Sludic. "What would you like me to report about Alia?"

"What can you report? You've just said you don't know who she is. Your chiefs believe she's an alien. I suspect they think she's an Auld!" Sludic laughed. "They'll prefer to go on thinking that. It suits their preconceptions. They'd have grabbed her if they could. But they couldn't—and now that she's left Earth they know they've lost her."

"How do my chiefs know about Alia? Are you accusing me of telling them?" Katina was half on her feet.

Sludic waved her back to her seat. "Of course

not! But why should you feel guilty if you had? That's your job isn't it?"

"I never report my impressions during a mission. I always wait until the end, and then report the facts. The way I've been taught."

"And you give your loyalty to the organization into which you've been infiltrated as long as the mission lasts. That's pushed you into acts you'd prefer to forget. They were justified by results. Nobody you've worked with has ever suspected you of being somebody else's agent, have they?"

Katina said nothing but her mouth clamped tight.

"Stop needling her, Sada! And how could you know such things?"

"We have taps into every major computer system on Earth." Sludic carelessly tossed off the most important item of information that Bose had heard since meeting him. "If you two want Terran systems to go on working smoothly, don't mention those taps to anyone else. Because if you do you'll bring most human activities to a confused halt!"

Bose drew back from another ethical squeeze, and shifted the problem. "Is Alia an Auld? A renegade? Give me a straight answer, or I'll know she is!"

"Unfortunately, Alex, Alia is not an Auld. I

don't know what she is. If I ever find out I promise I'll tell you."

"If we're still around to hear!" said Katina. "How old is she? How old are you?"

"Much older than you are, young lady. And much younger than you think I am. The same is true of Alia."

"So she can't be human?"

"That doesn't follow. On Earth you are a short-lived race. In healthier environments?" Sludic shrugged. "Who knows? But it's not as important as you assume. Subjective time and objective time are not the same and they flow at different rates. Even here on Earth. Things happen fast on this world. On your moon subjective time did not exist until men landed and brought unpredictability with them. Until life arrives on a planet everything that happens there is completely predictable. And subjective time is a function of uncertainty. The measure of subjective time is the number of unpredictable events that occur within the time unit. I have only been on Earth ninety days but, to me, that seems like ninety years."

"Objectively—how old?" Katina insisted.

"I have been hunting Alia since Sirius went nova."

"Sirius hasn't gone nova!"

"You haven't seen it yet so—as far as you're concerned—it hasn't. One cannot evade what your Einstein called general relativity. Sirius is in another system so arguing about when it went nova is arguing about the meaning of words. The same is true about my objective age. The Transits shift time as well as energy and matter. On a long transit time displacement is appreciable. Do you think we Auld are immortal? Far from it, thank God! I mean your God. Other worlds, other gods, other times! But yet time is as universal as the God of the Universe. When he made time he made plenty of it. And many varieties."

The mention of "God," as other than an oath, made both Katina and Bose uncomfortable. That was not hypothesis either of them cared to consider. Katina avoided the abstraction. "What do you mean? Different times?"

"Transit theory involves a gigantic paradox. We accept it because Transits work. You accept the paradox of intelligent life although, logically, it is so unlikely as to be absurd." Sludic shrugged. "The paradox of time is that it can be experienced but not investigated. We have to accept what we don't understand."

"Are you trying to say the living things in different parts of the Arm live to different clocks?"

Sludic nodded.

"Would humans who went there live to those clocks also?"

"Objectively it might be longer. Subjectively—there is probably little difference."

"You're saying that living longer makes no difference?"

"Very little." Sludic studied them. "Most humans won't believe that. If they thought that traveling the Transits could bring longevity—and were free to travel—they would go rushing away from Earth. And Earth would become a poor depopulated planet before they found they were wrong." He hesitated. "When we first discovered the Transits we rushed out along them and became emeshed in time paradoxes, for which we can now correct. By the time we had learned how to correct—"

"You didn't know how to get the loot back home?"

"Alia exaggerated. She has a habit of exaggerating."

"Paradoxes or not—I'd still like to ride the Transits," said Katina.

"Join the staff of the Transit Authority, and you will."

"Are you trying to bribe us with a promise of longevity?" asked Bose.

"You, Alex, are above bribery. And it is not a hunger for prolonged youth that is tempting Katina. It's her curiosity."

"Sada—why are you telling us so much after previously telling us so little? Are you snaring us with knowledge? If some others—Katina's chiefs, for example—think we know about Transits, then we'll be in the same danger that Alia was."

"It was Alia who forced this discussion on me. It was she who put you in peril by telling you so much this morning. For your own safety I have had to tell you more. My best guarantee of your silence is your realization that your personal safeties demand you reveal everything to your chiefs—or that you reveal nothing. And I know your mettle! You will not betray Alia and endanger Peter by repeating what you have learned."

"How can you believe that?" demanded Katina. "We're both loyal to Earth!"

"And so you will stay silent! Now you realize that—for the present—publishing what you know would harm humanity."

"Sada, people must decide for themselves."

"I agree. After they have been fully informed. Decisions based on incomplete information are likely to be faulty. And you do not have complete information. Even if you had, neither the general population of Earth nor your leaders would be able to understand it. Not at present. In the future perhaps—" He spread his hands. "So best be silent about the partial truth you know."

Bose was silent—for the moment. He watched

Katina start on her dessert. She must lead a tremendously energetic life to eat like she does and keep the figure she has. Presently she pushed her plate away and looked at Sludic. "What about Quine? He has a stake-out on Thalia's house."

The Marshal considered. "Gerald Quine is an efficient and dedicated officer. If I terminate his assignment abruptly he will be frustrated and suspicious. It would be wiser for me to let him decide for himself that Ruth Adams cannot be found. I will arrange for him to continue his investigation and report his progress at intervals."

Katina laughed. "A series of negative reports? He'll hate that!"

Bose was alarmed "What if he goes after Peter Ward?"

"I will give him strict instructions to stay away from Professor Ward. Quine has his faults, but he does as he is told. Unlike certain other officers with whom I have worked." The Marshal stood up. "Now, if you have quite finished eating, let us go." As they rose he added, "My offer of friendship remains open. To both of you."

Gerald Quine stared moodily at the "For Sale" sign on the front lawn of his quarry's late house. The tricky bitch! She'd never come back here, although he had been told by that fellow from Washington that she was on her way back. Somebody had slipped up. Probably that fat little doctor. Too many amateurs on this operation. Ruth Adams had somehow learned that the police were after her and had gone to ground. She hadn't learned it from any of his people—nor from Plastiras. An arrogant young woman, but an efficient officer. He gave her credit for knowing her job.

He had spent an unprofitable morning with Ruth Adams' lawyer. He'd leaned on the mouthpiece but the man hadn't sounded. Obviously had a cut in whatever the larceny was. Quine had investigated the lawyer's background and found nothing he could use as leverage. The man had prattled about "lawyer-client confidentiality" and tried to say that the Adams woman had taken a vow of poverty so she could enter some kind of a convent.

A convent would be a good hiding place. The history of crime was full of examples where men and women had taken cover behind some religious racket. The lawyer had refused to give even a hint as to which particular religious racket his client was using.

The only factual information Quine had been able to obtain was that the house and grounds had been deeded to the academic in Ithaca. And the man from Washington had specifically ordered him not to contact the Professor nor to investigate him in any way. Those loafers in ivory towers were a protected species!

But the fact that she had passed her loot on to her lover suggested an obvious conspiracy. An old trick! Put the cash in the name of an associate so that it would be hard to recover when she was caught and convicted of whatever she had done. A legal strategy designed to frustrate justice. That seemed to be the principal interest of the lawyers—to frustrate justice.

He would catch her! When he did she would tell him what she had done to have so many organizations after her. The whole operation had taken on the nature of a race. A race he, Gerald Quine, must win. His pride and his professional reputation were at stake. And he had been told to stay on her trail, to continue the operation. Careful attention to detail. That was the way that always worked in the end. It was only by going through the real estate records that he had found the house had been transferred to Peter Ward. Crooks did make slip-ups. Funds can be shifted privately, laundered, disguised in a dozen ways. But real estate transfers were always recorded in public records. For those who took the trouble to look.

Quine squared his shoulders and turned his back on the house. Attention to detail! The first detail must be a careful inspection of the photographs of airline passengers. With that hair the woman would be easy to pick out. She might cover it with a scarf but she wouldn't dye or cut it. Women were always being betrayed by their female vanity!

XII

It was a dull March morning when Sludic called and Bose reacted with nervous pleasure to the Marshal's voice. "Sada! What are you doing back on Earth?"

"I've hardly left your damned planet since last fall. I want you and Katina out here, right away!"

"I'll have to get clearance. And—"

"I've already spoken to your Director General. You're assigned to me. Full time liaison. He's the only human who'll know—except Katina. She's waiting for you now. Outside your main entrance. In her Ford."

"You mustn't involve Katina—"

"She's a Transit employee. Joined the Transit service on orders from her own Chiefs. She'll drive you to the Terminal."

"Sada, what's all this about?"

"You'll know when you get here! Alex, start moving!" And the Marshal hung up.

His colloquial English has improved and his manners have deteriorated, thought Bose as he went to the elevator. Yet he would enjoy meeting Sludic again. It had been a lonely winter. Few friends; none among his colleagues.

And it would be good to see Katina. The only human who knew about Alia. The only person with whom he could exchange ideas about the Auld. She waved to him when he came out of the UN and opened the door of her Ford. "Jump in. We're back in business."

"What business?" He paused, suddenly alarmed. "Katina, if we go into Transit territory Sludic'll be able to do what he likes with us."

"I work for the Authority now. Service orders!" She laughed. "Never been allowed through the barrier so far. Hope they'll let us in today." She tried to quiet Bose's apprehension. "Sludic swore he was calling on us because he wanted our help. Not to harm us."

He got in beside her, partly relieved. "But you thought he might?"

"We're the pair of humans who know too much." She accelerated toward the thruway.

"In my business people who know too much tend to be terminated." The car rocked as she swung around a bend. "But that's not the Marshal's way."

"Why has he sent for us so suddenly? Why is he back on Earth? And why was he so rude?"

"I could make a guess. But I won't."

"You know something?"

"A little."

"And it's better I don't!" He sighed, wishing he was back fighting the battles he was trained to fight. Against dirt, disease, and death. Not up against an opponent with whom he was half in sympathy. Wishing that he had the self-confidence of this young woman, almost young enough to be his daughter. "Where's Peter Ward?"

"In cloud-cuckoo-land! Cruising the Aegean in a rented yacht. Digging up the dirt on Pallas Athene. Spending Thalia's money on the damnedest things. He thinks of her as some kind of a goddess."

"A goddess? If only I were superstitious enough to believe that! It would explain everything." He also wished that Katina would drive slower; they had joined the flow of traffic thundering toward the Terminal and she was dodging semitrailers.

"Thalia's no goddess!" said Katina with

conviction. "She may be something else. Her full name's Thalia. Know who Thalia was?"

"One of the Muses, wasn't she?"

"A Grace and a Muse. The Muse of comedy. Our Thalia has a certain sense of humor. If she reined it in she wouldn't fall into the shit so often."

"Is she in trouble now?"

"Perhaps. Sludic sure is—from the way he spoke to me."

"He was curt." Bose's heart sank. Thalia— Alia—was the only thing that had angered the Marshal in the past.

Up the turnoff toward the Administration buildings. As before—they were expected. The gate rose. Up the hill. Transit territory. How long before they'd be allowed out? The alien atmosphere closed on them.

Katina parked by the entrance. "There's the Marshal. Waiting for us. He's really uptight! Come on, Alex—you're the rep for the top man on Earth. He's just a Transit Commissioner. Runs a kind of railroad." But she was as nervous as he when Sludic strode toward them.

The Marshal was wearing the loose combat coveralls of a Transit Guard and the lines of worry on his usually calm face made him seem entirely human. So did his brusque greeting. "Alex, Katina. You've arrived at last! Leave the car and come inside!" He turned and walked toward the entrance.

They followed in his wake, attracting little attention from the figures in blue gowns or combat coveralls in the lobby and passages. "They think we're just another pair of pseudo-humans returning from a night's spying!" murmured Katina. "Not too hard to fool!"

"For God's sake, don't try to fool the Marshal. He's in no mood for humor."

They went down a series of corridors, past rooms filled with control panels and displays, under their feet the hum of tremendous machines. Machines sunk deep into the hill. Machines that powered the Transit. They were probably the first humans to have been allowed into this high-tech anthill. Anthill—a description that would delight his colleagues back in the UN.

Auld everywhere, all looking somewhat human in their loose clothes. They learn enough English to talk to us, and make themselves look sufficiently like us not to be repulsive, thought Bose. Thoughtful of them to take the trouble. A lot of extra work to avoid hurting human susceptibilities. Some of Bose's ancestors had never taken much trouble to avoid hurting the susceptibilities of his other ancestors.

Sludic was leading them into the heart of

Transit control. After seeing this would he ever let them out? Or would they be pushed out God knows where? Bose was sweating gently when the Marshal opened a door and said, "Here's my office. Come on in."

The reverse of what Bose had expected. A senior executive's office, much like Bose's own. Vast desk, deep carpet, leather chairs, telephones, terminals, cadenza for liquor, bland pictures on the walls. "I keep it this way to avoid culture-shock when I go among the natives!" He caught Bose's eye. "That's a joke, Alex!" He dropped into a senior-executive chair behind the desk and waved Katina and Bose to junior-executive chairs in front of it. Then he leaned forward across it. "Alia's on the loose again!"

"Good for Thalia!" said Katina.

"This time I mean to kill her!" snapped Sludic.

"If you can catch her!" said Katina.

Bose recovered from his shock and broke in, "Alia said you'd have killed her last time, if you'd caught her when you first arrived. And that— well—your conscience would have troubled—"

"This time I'll risk the guilt." The Marshal paused. "I think she's back on Earth."

"Tell us where—so we can help her stay here," said Katina.

"When this is over, Miss Plastiras, I'll have your balls!"

Katina laughed. Bose murmured, "Sada, I've warned you before! Don't try to be crude. You end up being funny."

"I've been contaminated by your damned culture!" Sludic cracked his knuckles.

"What happened? The last time we saw her she was surrounded by Guards."

"Guards by courtesy. Incompetents, in fact," said Katina.

Sludic again cracked his knuckles. "They took her to Gada for questioning. No, it was not rough, although the Directors are very interested in finding how much she knows that she shouldn't. They congratulated me on catching her." He scowled at Katina. "You can imagine how popular I'll be with the Directors if they learn she's escaped again."

"But they did question her?"

"They questioned her! I suspect she learned more from them than they did from her. What they did extract was another demonstration of her ingenuity. Somehow or other she got hold of a Guard rig—complete with helmet. After the final session she left with eight Guards. There were nine Guards when they arrived at her quarters. As all nine had passed the barriers there was confusion about who was what. By the time the squad had sorted themselves out there were eight Guards and no prisoner."

"Bunch of clowns!" remarked Katina. "Remember why I was chary of joining your organization, Marshal?"

Sludic's knuckles cracked louder. Bose was so alarmed by the Marshal's rising anger that he hissed, "If you interrupt again, Miss Plastiras, I will strangle you with my bare hands!" Then he slumped back in his chair, astounded by his own action and astounding Katina and Sludic by his eruption out of character. "Where did she go?"

Sludic recovered. "First, to Larga. Where we had planned to send her anyway. I assumed she had anticipated her transfer only to show us how clever she is."

"The Muse of Comedy at it again!" murmured Katina, then she flinched at Bose's glare.

"Muse of Comedy?" Sludic was easily diverted. He keyed his terminal and read the answer. "Ah! Thalia! You think that's significant?"

"Perhaps!" said Bose wearily. "Is she still there?"

"We don't think so. The place is crawling with intellectuals of every race and shape. We haven't checked on them all. But my guess is she took off when we closed in. We picked up a faint trail leading toward the hub."

"You said you thought she was back on Earth."

"The trail was faint enough to be genuine. Now I think it was fake. A trickster trail!" Sludic pulled on his lower lip; he seemed to have acquired a variety of human tics. "She led half my squads off on a wild goose chase. What the hell is a wild goose chase, Alex?"

"I've no idea!" Bose was as baffled by Sludic's shift of subject as by his question.

"A kind of horse race," said Katina. "The rider in the lead picked the course and the others had to follow. So it went all over the place—the way a flock of wild geese suddenly shifts direction. Once a rider had established a lead he was very difficult to catch. So they gave it up as a form of racing." She smiled at Sludic. "An appropriate metaphor for Thalia's tactics."

"Why do you think she's come back to Earth?" persisted Bose, anxious to keep Sludic's attention away from Katina. "As you've pointed out in the past, she's liable to be trapped here."

"Why back to Earth? Because Peter Ward is here. He's her friend."

"He's her lover. Or was!" Katina seemed determined to hold the floor. "There's a difference between friends and lovers. Friends last longer!"

"Among us, friendships last forever." Sludic

made an irritated gesture, as though he realized how often he was being turned away from the line of discussion. "You're her friends too, but Peter was her partner. She risked Pirenne's thugs when she picked him up in Ithaca. From what I have read about human romances she'll want to renew her relationship with Peter. He was her first love, and that is always the strongest among you humans."

"You've been reading too many paperback romances!" said Katina.

"I found them fascinating and informative."

"You would!" Katina paused. "I think she's doubled back because she enjoys taking risks. When she spoke to me on the phone—"

"When she what?" Sludic was on his feet.

"Spoke on the phone. Last December. Said she was visiting."

"Telephoned you?" Sludic came around his desk and towered over her. "Last December. What for?"

"To wish me a Happy Christmas. And ask if anybody was hassling Peter." Katina was staring up at the Marshal with the expression of a child who had poked a tiger with a stick and is hoping it is safely caged.

"Visiting? Visiting where?"

"Earth, of course."

"Why didn't you report her call?"

"Why should I? She hasn't broken any Terran laws. And I'm her attorney. Client-lawyer conversations are privileged." She eased back in her chair, her eyes on Sludic's face. "Anyway, your operation on Earth was over. Or so you told us. I assumed you'd taken pity on her and let her come home."

"Pity on Alia?" In his effort to remain rational Sludic's voice became so cold that Bose shivered and Katina flinched. "Did you tell Peter Ward that she was on Earth?"

"No. She particularly asked me not to. I think she's still fond of Peter. But I don't think she's going to risk her neck going after him. As I said, lovers are transient. Mine are, anyway."

Sludic was on the verge of asking her to explain her last comment when Bose cut in, "Did you tell anyone?"

"Of course not! Thalia's my client. And my friend."

Sludic strode up and down the office, returned to glare down at Katina. "It is fortunate for you, young lady, that my humanity is only skin-deep. That I am still essentially an Auld and a Marshal. Were I human I would hand you over to Quine."

"Sada," Bose protested, not trusting that Sludic's humanity was as shallow as he claimed. "You swore us to secrecy when you left Earth. And you didn't leave any forwarding address."

Sludic turned toward him. "I'm sure your combined skills could have got a message to me through the Embassy."

"But she doesn't have confidential access to the Embassy—"

The Marshal cut him off with an oath that was definitely Earthy. "Katina uses her Service computer to learn all kinds of things she's not supposed to know. Don't you, girl?" He turned back to Katina who seemed more abashed by that accusation than anything said earlier.

"Sada?" Bose was desperate to avoid the explosion he felt was imminent. "Why did you bring us here?"

"I'll tell you that when I'm again rational!" And he turned on his heel and strode out of the office.

"For God's sake, stop it!" Bose hissed at Katina. "You may find it amusing to taunt him. You don't know the danger—to both of us! If he'd been any other Marshal you'd be dead by now. Me too, maybe!"

"I wasn't trying to raise laughs!" She looked down at her hands, which were shaking. "I was trying to make him mad. Did better than I planned."

"Make him mad? Why? When I was trying to calm him down!"

"Because when the Auld get mad they stop being rational. Thalia told me—and showed me. That confrontation! You heard how he grabbed at any chance remark to get away from the subject. Typical flight of ideas!" She pressed her hands to her face. "I wasn't amused. I was scared shitless!"

Bose considered her theory while she recovered her composure. It was true that Sludic had flung from the room without asking the obvious question. Had Thalia called her again? Had the two women met? Finally he said, "I think you've pushed him far enough!"

"So do I!" She smiled weakly.

Sludic came back into the room. "I apologize for my behavior. Why did I bring you two out here?" He sat down behind his desk. "Because I still prefer to take Alia alive. There have been moments in the past when I might have killed her had I caught her. I have always been able to resist the temptation. Now, I am no longer confident of my own restraint. When the Directors hear of her escape—!" He gripped the edge of his desk, his knuckles white.

"And you want us with you to act as your conscience?" Katina leaned forward. "Marshal, I understand your feelings. If I'd been in your shoes I'd have shot her the first time I had her in my sights."

"Yes—you would. But you are human. I am not. And Alia was right when she said an agony of guilt would follow—for me." He looked at Bose. "Alex—you showed me *Les Miserables*. I remember what happened to Javert in the end."

"What did?" asked Katina.

"He drowned himself. Young lady, you should be more familiar with your own great literature."

"My French isn't very good."

Oh God, she's starting to divert him again, thought Bose. "How can we keep you from such a tragedy?"

"I hope I will be too ashamed to be brutal—if you are with me." Sludic stood up, and added briskly, "Also, you are Alia's only friends on Earth. The only people she can turn to for help. So, until she is taken, I am going to keep you by me. You will become members of my squad."

Bose gaped. Katina started to speak. "If I may—"

Sludic cut her off. "No, you may not attempt to improve its efficiency by introducing your Special Service techniques. My Guards are not yet down to the level at which they could use them effectively." He pressed a button on the edge of his desk and an Auld in combat gear, looking more human than most, came into the room. "This is Gerdin. The equivalent of a Quartermaster-Sergeant. He will show you your rooms where you will find complete Guard kits—less blasters, of course. Please change into them now. The squad is on stand-by. My flier is waiting. We may take off at any time. That is why I brought you here in haste. Gerdin will provide you with a meal when you have changed."

Katina stood up. "Aren't we going to have any say—"

"No, Katina. For once there is nothing you can say."

XIII

Peter pulled himself over the edge of the cliff and lay panting on the coarse grass of the promontory. The sun had gone down behind Psara's single peak and the remains of the temple were in shadow, but above him the gulls were still flashing in the last light. It had been a hard climb from the beach and the weight of his rucksack had made it harder. He slipped the straps from his shoulders, rolled over, and sat up. Then he glanced back down and shuddered.

The captain of the yacht had thought him crazy. He probably was crazy. He got to his feet, picked up his rucksack, and walked to where the two pillars of the temple rose against the darkening sky. His whole pilgrimage was a crazy, last-minute decision. And trying to reach the temple by the most direct—and most difficult—route had been the craziest of all. But that was how a pilgrim should approach a shrine, and it was the route Thalia had used a year before.

He looked around him; at the ruined temple, at the mountain rising above it, at the sea below, and knew his intuition had been right. This was no shrine of Aphrodite's and never had been. The orientation validated his theory and showed this place was sacred to Pallas Athene, born from the sea, the goddess of the azure eyes, the Preserver of Cities.

One of the earliest of Athene's temples. Her shrine had been here long before the Doric pillars had been raised. Somewhere nearby, probably up one of the narrow ravines running back into the mountain, was the cave and spring which would have been her original sanctuary. He would search for it in the morning. Tonight he could only sit on the fallen stones and watch the dusk sweeping in across the Aegean, enjoying in gentle melancholy the memories which haunted him from the year before.

He had come to Greece determined to keep them free of later overlays; to preserve untarnished his first image of Thalia. He had chartered a twenty-meter power yacht and cruised among the Cyclades: from Syros to Paros to sacred Delos, while the captain had complained about the danger of storms so early in the season. "But the time for seafaring has arrived," Peter had said. "In two days the Pleiades will be rising with the sun."

The captain had stared blankly at him, then started to protest when, seized by an impulse, he had added, "Take me to Psara."

The captain had continued to protest, not so much from fear of the equinoctial gales as from the danger to a real-estate deal he had set up on Mytelene. But Peter had been insistent. "Put me ashore on Psara tomorrow."

They had arrived off Psara late on a fine spring afternoon. Peter had pointed to the rocky beach at the base of the cliffs beneath the temple promontory. "Land me there. Then go round to the harbor and tie up for the night. I'll be back aboard some time tomorrow."

The mate, a muscular young woman, had rowed him ashore in the dinghy and when she had got back to the yacht had stood with the captain watching the American start his climb. "He is mad!" the captain had said.

"He is a poet!" remarked the mate, as if that explained everything.

"A mad poet and a poor mountaineer!" the captain had spun the wheel, turning the yacht toward the headland and the harbor beyond. "He will probably break his neck!"

The mate had looked wistfully at the dot crawling up the cliff face. Such a handsome young man! Why were such men always obsessed with searching for things they would never find?

Peter had not broken his neck, and was wondering why he had risked it. For one thing it was growing cold now the sun had disappeared. For another, it was lonely, even lonelier than the year before. And this time no goddess would sing to him when the sun rose. He sat down on one of the fallen stones and pulled a flask of brandy from his rucksack. The liquor warmed his stomach and increased his melancholy.

He had tried to persuade himself that the only reason for this dash to Psara was to test his hypothesis that the temple had been dedicated to Pallas Athene by checking its orientation against the dawn stars on the morning when the Pleiades rose with the sun. He knew that the real reason he had come was nostalgia, the romantic need to mourn his lost love at the place and time he had first met her. After brooding for a while he unrolled his sleeping bag and laid it out in one of the hollows of the site of the temple. Then he crawled into it, intending to lie on his back and watch the constellations wheel overhead, but the combination of weariness and brandy only let him stay awake long enough to set his watch-alarm for an hour before dawn. As he fell asleep he heard the puttering of a minicopter out over the sea. Some fool was making a night crossing from Chios.

Awake she might never come to him, but asleep she came to him constantly. Sleeping amid the ruins of her temple he saw her striding toward him from among the stars. Her helmet pushed back from her face, her azure eyes flashing, the aegis as her breastplate, her spear in her hand, coming to the rescue of her people. His awe and his desire were so strong that he sat up, reaching out toward her, and then found himself awake in the hollow among the stones of her ancient temple.

The constellations showed it was close to midnight, the moon had not yet risen, and the pillars were barely visible against the night sky. Half-asleep and shaking from the intensity of his dream, he looked around and at first saw nothing but black shadows. Then one shadow moved. A shadow that was the outline of a helmeted figure, silhouetted against the stars.

Peter scrambled to his feet, grabbed his flash, and flooded the shadow with light. The figure swung around, its hand coming up, and Peter froze with terror as he saw Thalia's face, glowing with fury as it had glowed in his dream. Her hand pointed directly at him. He fell into darkness.

He drifted back to consciousness with her face floating above him, framed by her helmet. "Athena!" he gasped.

"What the hell are you talking about?" said the face.

The words shocked him back to consciousness. He tried to sit up, found he was too weak, and flopped back onto the grass.

"Peter—what are you doing here?"

"I—I came to watch the Pleiades rise with the sun. As we did last year. Are you—are you—?"

"Am I what?"

He stared up at her and blurted out, "Are you a goddess?"

She was kneeling beside him, her gaze so intense that he raised his hand to shield his eyes. She caught his fingers and gently moved them away from his face. "Where did you get that crazy idea?"

"You look like Pallas Athene. You act like her. And you struck me down."

"Sorry about that. I heard something move and when I turned, you blinded me with your flash. So I hit you." She pressed his hand. "You'll be okay in a few minutes." The softness suddenly went from her voice. "Are you alone?"

"I was!"

"How did you get here?"

"Climbed the cliff. From the beach."

"You what? Peter—you're crazy!" She paused, looking down at him with worried affection. "Were you followed?"

"No." He managed to sit up.

"How can you be sure?"

He told her about the chartered power-yacht and his last-minute decision to come to Psara. When he had finished she seemed satisfied. "Then we're probably safe. For tonight at any rate."

"Safe from what?"

"I'll tell you that later. Is your strength coming back?"

"I think so." He clambered to his feet and looked around, reassuring himself that he was still among the ruins of the temple, that the woman with him was indeed Thalia. The moon had risen while he had been unconscious and he could see her clearly. She was dressed in the kind of coveralls worn by the Transit Guard and was wearing a Guard helmet. While he watched she slipped if off and shook out her hair, turning to silver by the moonlight. "What are you doing in that rig?"

"Getting out of it!" She shed her coveralls and then started to unzip her jumpsuit. "Peter, are you strong enough to make love?"

He stared at her, moon-struck. Her jumpsuit fell to her ankles and she stood naked before him, her body white under the moon, her beauty more than mortal. Then, once again, desire swamped awe, and he took her in his arms, pulling her down onto his sleeping bag.

After their first hot encounter the night chilled them. He pressed her against him and whispered. "Thalia—who are you? Why are you here? Katina said you'd left Earth." When she didn't answer he squeezed her. "Are you mortal?"

"Ouch! My ribs are! Peter—of course I'm human." She kissed him with a slow passion. "Doesn't that prove it?"

"A human who's been wandering around the Arm for millennia?"

"Who told you that?" Her voice was suddenly sharp.

"Nobody. Just intuition—and logic. You've been off-Earth, and you were off it for a long time."

"Peter, I may have been off Earth. But I'm as human as you are."

"For nearly three thousand years?"

"Time isn't the same everywhere. Or rather, it flows at a different rate. Okay—I'm older than I look. And act! Until you jumped me I thought I'd recovered my good sense." She sighed, then snuggled up against him. "But I'm glad I lost it. For tonight at any rate. Let's enjoy our foolishness!"

He caught her seeking hand. "You've got to tell me the truth!"

"Why?" She reached out for him again.

Again he checked her. "Why not?" He sensed her anger but he did not flinch. "Why won't you tell me who you are?"

"I warned you before. Too dangerous!"

He took her chin and tipped up her face. "Something you're ashamed of?"

She pushed him away. "I'm ashamed of falling in love with a dreamy-eyed romantic who prefers myth to reality!"

"Thalia—with things as they are, it's good sense to prefer myth. Reality's too damned unpleasant. I'd hoped you'd come back to alter that."

Her eyes flashed in the moonlight. "What makes you think I've been away so long?"

"Sappho's ode. The way you speak Aeolic Greek—that's answered a dozen questions about its syntax. And other things. Things only somebody interested in preclassical Greek history would recognize. Katina suspects something, but she doesn't know enough to do more than suspect." He squeezed her again. "Don't worry! I'm about the only classicist under sixty who could pick them up. I kept my mouth shut about Sappho. I'll keep it shut about you. But you can't leave me half-demented again. So tell me the truth."

She looked up into his face and stroked his hair. "I can't leave you half-demented. But you must promise not to repeat what I tell you. It might be dangerous—as I warned you before. Though after today I hope it won't be so important." She hesitated. "Anyway, my story's so weird that nobody's going to believe you, even if you did repeat it. Even you may not believe it."

"I will believe it. And I won't repeat it." He kissed her.

"Darling Peter! Then keep quiet and listen!"

First, as I told you, I am human. Perhaps enhanced human. I won't weary you with theories. Accept my word for what I am.

I speak Aeolic Greek because that's my mother tongue. I was born on this little island about thirty years after your Sappho died on Mytelen. No questions, Peter! Not yet.

My father's house stood where the village is now; in his household were more people than are in the village today. And, as you suggested, this temple was dedicated not to Aphrodite but to Pallas Athene. It was already derelict. Athena was not a popular goddess in these islands.

There was still one priestess, but she was almost senile. There had once been many serving Athena's temple and shrine, but they had disappeared one by one and Arthis was the last and alone.

I was no goddess but only a romantic girl of thirteen. I used to bring her fruit and flowers, not so much as a tribute to Athena, whom even then I considered an especially bloody-minded deity, but because Arthis, while technically still a virgin and so qualified to be a priestess, had as a young girl been among Sappho's lovers and used to sing me Sappho's songs.

There were few other worshippers and had it not been for me Arthis would have starved. My father was a kind and religious man, and though Poseidon was the patron deity of our house, he approved of what he thought were signs of piety in his frivolous daughter. So I used to come up here and listen to Arthis recite Sappho and tell me tales of gods, goddesses, and mortals. Of spirits, ghosts, and the underworld.

Most of them were too wild for even a girl of thirteen to believe, but one did ring true; her account of how her predecessors had left. As was not true of her other stories, she had seen it happen. In fact she claimed she had watched all the priestesses who had been serving the temple when she was a young woman go, in their turn, through the gateway that led to Elysium or the Underworld. As each one had grown too feeble to perform the rituals, she had gone to Athena's shrine, a cave up that ravine, on a night when Orion was due to pass directly above it. She had prayed alone in the cave while the others prayed outside. Then, at the moment when Orion's sword had come over the rim of the ravine, her prayers had stopped, and when the others had gone inside they had found the cave empty.

Arthis had seen this happen eight times until she, who had been the youngest, was now the oldest and alone. She was angered by my youthful skepticism and took me up to show me the shrine, warning me never to enter when Orion was high in the heavens.

As you once said, all over Greece, all around the Mediterranean, there are so-called entrances to the Underworld. We were fascinated by Hades. I was fascinated myself. I invoked her gratitude for the food I brought to make her promise that when the time came for her to go she would let me watch her leave. She probably interpreted that as a threat, but she agreed on condition that I care for Athena's temple after she was gone.

A few weeks later she decided her time had come; perhaps because she had, at last, shifted responsibility for the temple onto somebody else. I brought her food one evening and found her waiting in the ravine. She waved toward the stars, mumbled a series of senseless injunctions, and then hobbled into the cave. I, instead of staying in the ravine as the priestesses had always done, settled down outside the cave to see what would actually happen.

She sat on a rock with her flickering oil lamp at her feet, singing a hymn to Athena. Halfway through her voice cut off, her lamp went out, and looking up I saw that the three brilliant stars of Orion's Belt were above me.

I remained frozen with fear until they had swung past the ravine, and then crept into the cave. Arthis and her lamp had disappeared. There was not a trace of them. I ran all the way home and got whipped for being out so late.

I didn't dare tell my parents what I had promised because I had, in effect, dedicated myself to Pallas Athene and, not only did my father disapprove of Athena as the enemy of Poseidon, but he had already arranged my marriage to a handsome young man, the heir to an estate on Chios. A marriage which I was eagerly awaiting. However that marriage was a year away and I continued to come up to the temple and make token sacrifices in the hope that Athena would have forgotten my promise by the time I married and deserted her shrine.

Arthis left in the spring. That summer the Athenians came in their swift ships on a punitive expedition against our island. Democratic Athens was a brutal enemy, as Athena was a cruel goddess. I was up at her temple when I saw the smoke rising from beyond the cliffs and ran to look down and see my father and brothers killed, our house looted and burned, my mother and sisters led away into slavery. Of the six hundred in my father's house I was the only one not dead or enslaved. I was alone up here, starving and close to madness.

There were many myths of humans visiting the Underworld; virgins are supposed to be allowed to enter Hades on certain missions. I knew of an entrance and I was a virgin. Light-headed with grief and hunger I decided I would follow my father and my brothers, but not through the Door of Death. I would go alive, so I would not be one of Pluto's subjects and could plead with him to release at least my father. It was not a particularly courageous decision when my only alternatives were starvation or slavery.

I managed to exist on roots and fruit until Orion was again due to swing above the ravine. I crept into the cave as Arthis had done, and sat where she had sat. I went as she had gone. And dropped into what I immediately recognized as Hell.

In fact I had been sucked through the equalizing aperture of a natural transit, one of the rifts through which temporal parity is maintained, one that happened to have a periodicity coincident with the swing of Orion. It was from such rifts in the infrastructure of space that the Auld learned how to drive their tunnels from world to world. I dropped across infraspace into a horrible world populated by monsters. An oxygen world, so I could breathe and eat but where, had I been larger, I would soon have been eaten.

That must have happened to most living beings who fell through the transit. That had probably been the fate of Athena's priestesses. The inhabitants of that world-without-a-name are savage omnivores; the degenerate descendants of what must have once been a technologically advanced but always brutal race. They captured me as I wandered, skinny and starving. The band that caught me kept me. First perhaps as a kind of pet, perhaps to fatten up. They took me with them on their raids, and those raids were, for them, successful so they kept me as a mascot.

They are an abominable people, skilled in war but little else. And because they know of the network of natural fissures which connects a number of worlds beyond civilization, they could raid other barbarian peoples. And they took me with them.

For how long I have no real idea. Out there you live to a different clock. Physically I was about sixteen when they raided a world with

signs of civilization. And where some of the captured inhabitants, before they were butchered,
seemed to recognize me. I assumed there must
be men on this world and I escaped to find
them. Escape was not hard. I had been traveling with the war party for what seemed a
lifetime and had become as skilled as any of
my captors, although a good deal smaller.

I did not find men; I found Auld. When I
saw them I thought at first they were humans
like myself, as did the locals I had captured
and forced to act as my guides. But when I
reached what I now know was a Transit Terminal, I found they only superficially resem-
bled men.

There were two of them and they didn't
know what to make of me, but they accepted
me into their Terminal and treated me kindly.
And when my late captors came tracking their
mascot and demanded its return to be barbecued, the two Auld destroyed all of them easily.

The Transit Authority had driven a transit
to that fringe world and had left the two Guards
to operate a trading post for a trial period. At
first, like the savages, the two treated me as a
kind of pet and then, after I had learned the
basics of their language, as a barbarian companion. That would have been unthinkable almost anywhere else in the Arm, but those two
had been left alone for a long, long time and

were already a little senile when I arrived. When I began to dress like an Auld, talk like an Auld, and even think like an Auld they assumed I was an Auld and I gradually became a member of a Triad, a group which most Auld prefer to a Duo. And, as a member of a Triad I helped to operate the Terminal.

Time and aging are different out there, as I mentioned earlier. I matured while they became decrepit. They knew they would never be relieved, because the post had not prospered and it was their duty to decay with their station. Happiness, for an Auld, is doing one's duty. The harder the happier. They are Spartans without the cruelty of Spartans. But they are as rigid and as dull.

When Otho died Ratho suffered. They dread loneliness. No Auld is expected to function alone for long. Had I not been there Ratho would have closed the Terminal, transmitted the final shipment, and then killed himself. But, in his dotage, he treated me as a young Auld and I gave him the companionship he needed. I gave it to him and learned all he knew. And what one Auld knows all Auld know. They are the ultimate egalitarians, equal in everything, and their ready cooperation, their easy agreement, their rapid consensus, makes them deathly dull, even to those few Auld who show individual initiative and so automatically rise to leadership. There is one Marshal called Sludic, the Marshal who is hunting me, who now prefers human company to the company of his fellows! I'll tell you more about him later.

Poor Ratho! Left to die alone on a fringe world. Auld cruelty may be unintended but it can be real. He assumed that after he died I would close the Terminal and kill myself in correct Auld fashion. When he did die I performed his funeral rites, collected the weapons and gear, signalled that the station was closing with the proper ceremonial signals, and left with the last shipment.

I found myself free to wander among the worlds served by the Transit Authority. I could talk like an Auld and, when correctly clothed, pass as one. Not, perhaps, on close inspection but I was never inspected closely. Only Auld can speak Auld so I had only to speak to be accepted without question. I knew the coding for the transits, I knew how to access Central Information, so I could find out what I wanted to know and travel where I liked. No Auld travels alone in combat gear except on duty, so when I went through the Terminals in combat gear the Guard knew I was traveling on duty.

But I was not. I was human and alone. My loneliness harried me; my humanity plagued me. At times I despised myself as a barbarian, and at times my humanity drove me into acting like one. I had, after all, seen my father and my brothers killed, my mother and sisters carried away into slavery. I had traveled with a brutal war party from world to world, preying off the inhabitants. I had come to realize that my own race was indeed barbarian. I could not abide dullness and boredom. I was goaded by the physical and emotional drives of a young woman.

I would stay for a time on some world where many intelligent races coexist, a world where I could shed my Auld disguise. But, sooner or later, I would become so frustrated that I would do something flamboyant, something that would call attention to myself. I was a unique wanderer, moving through various societies, living among peoples who had the company of their own kind and were performing worthwhile tasks. I had nobody of my own kind, and I had nothing worthwhile to do. I did not dare join in operating the Transits, the only work I knew and the only function the Auld perform. A function which includes controlling trade and policing the System.

It was some foolishness of mine which first brought that Marshal, Sludic, looking for me. By then, I suppose, my antics had been reported to the Auld elite, the Directors of Transit. They sent Sludic and his partner Radic to find out who I was and what I was doing. The pair tracked me across several worlds and by the time they caught up with me I had been living on Larga for some time, unnoticed among individuals from many different races. I was wearing a costume of my own design and did not appear the slightest bit Auldish. I was also bored to petulance.

The result was that when Sludic and Radic arrived to question me I amused myself, failing to realize that they were not a typical pair. It was only after several of their visits that I felt the game getting out of hand. By then I knew that if the Auld found I could pass as a Guard and speak their language, they would certainly isolate me and probably kill me. The pair were still typical enough to consult their seniors before acting, and when they returned to act I was gone. Sludic has learned a great deal more about how to hunt since that time. I have been both his quarry and his teacher. And somewhere, some time during the subsequent chase Radic must have been killed, for when I doubled back to observe my hunters I found Sludic was pursuing me alone.

For an Auld the death of a group member, especially a partner, is a tragedy that not all survive. I think Sludic blamed me for Radic's death; my capture seemed to become his obsession. And as he started to work alone he began to act faster and more decisively.

Speed in decision and action are rare talents

among the Auld, and that is probably the reason for his rise in the Transit Authority—he is now both Commissioner and Marshal. But despite his new duties he still had time to come after me whenever he got news of me.

For my part, I had become bored with the game and was already searching for Earth. I returned to Larga and settled there, this time taking care to remain unobtrusive. Another scholar in a community of scholars, scholars of every race, shape, and size. I appropriated a terminal and began to search for information about Earth. And though there was no world in the catalog of worlds which might be Earth, I found records of some artifacts which had so far defied classification: such things as weapons, vases, and ornaments which must have dropped through some natural rift and which I recognized as Terran. I made myself a specialist by starting to catalog them.

Almost every permanent resident on Larga is a cataloger. Imagine a world of librarians reading only enough of each book to decide how it should be referenced, with little interest in what it says. I was accepted without question. There were always vacancies for catalogers, even on Larga only so many individuals can continue in such boring tasks, and many of my colleagues looked even weirder to each other than I did to them. I grubbed out my own cell in that vast anthill by initiating a new classification address for data related to those artifacts, so that when information about others like them arrived it was automatically routed to me.

I could identify the rifts through which they had come, but that gave me no information about Earth's position in astrogeographical terms for the routes of natural and artificial transits through the infrastructure of space bear little relationship to steller geography. It was only when those Californians blasted their way into a transit that I discovered where Earth was. The Directorate queried Larga about the possible origin of the creatures and artifacts which had suddenly arrived at the Gaden junction. It was I who identified their world of origin as Earth and notified the Directorate that certain of the artifacts suggested a dangerously high-tech culture, that Earth was a world which must be investigated. After that I persuaded another scholar to take over my cell and expertise. I myself started out on my way home.

As soon as I began to move Sludic began to harry me. I had learned many useful skills on Larga—you, Peter, had experienced some of them! How to search for diamonds was another. I covered my trail and went first to Nuerth to discover more about modern humans, and accumulate the money I soon learned I would need to settle on Earth. On Nuerth I found diamonds, as I told you, and learned human ways and human languages. Then, at last, I came home. I came to settle down and find a lover. I searched for ten years—then I found you!

I am making all this sound easy; in some ways it was. The Auld do not lie and are un-skilled in deceit. They are too strong to have need of such things. They are so strong they can act with direct force and the least cruelty.

I was a young girl from a small island, a weak island. And the weak must lie and cheat to survive. I came from a people for whom the "wily Odysseus" was a hero. Armed with a blaster, in combat gear, I was as powerful as any Auld, and much stronger than any individual among the civilized races they rule. Yet I still retained the talents of the weak.

And the Auld are weakening slowly. Deteriorating slowly, as has every dominant race in human and Arm history, once it has secured dominance. It freezes into a specialized role and is broken when the environment changes. They need an infusion of vigor—perhaps my mischievous interference with their well-planned systems was an attempt to evoke something of their old spirit. For, when all is said and done, it would be a tragedy of cosmic dimensions if one of those savage races with whom I raided and fought, ever learn how to invade the transit system and find hundreds of peaceful worlds open to plunder.

I have reawakened something in the Auld. I was the kind of opponent they must have had to face long ago, but which they had forgotten existed. As they themselves have forgotten how to lie and deceive. I think Sada Sludic has learned a measure of deceit from me!

As I had been learning better behavior from him. Learned enough, perhaps, to grow tired of the game. Ashamed of myself, even. Started to yearn only to live quietly on Earth with a lover, grow old like a human. I thought I had achieved that aim. Until last summer.

Pirenne? No, Pirenne was a nuisance, nothing more. Last summer I learned that Sludic had tracked me to Earth, that he was still hunting me. More than that—he caught me! How? I'll not say. He would not make truces. His damned sense of duty! He shipped me off-Earth. I escaped, of course, and came back. He started after me again. He is hot on my trail now. His ship is probably high above us, scouring the Aegean. He's liable to catch me on this island.

XIV

"Like hell he will!" Peter was on his feet, staring up at the night sky.

"Relax!" She laughed and pulled him back down. "He won't do anything before dawn—even if he is up there. With all their gadgets the Auld don't like the dark. Even if he has followed me, we've still time left for love."

"I dreamed you were Pallas Athene, racing across the heavens to rescue your people!"

"Be glad I'm not! She wasn't much at protection! She let Athens get devastated by the Spartans, the Macedonians, the Romans, et cetera, and finally deteriorate into a village under the Turks. Her Athenians killed my father and brothers, enslaved my mother and sisters. If you want to fantasize a goddess, take Aphrodite! She's your real patroness!" She kissed him to prove her point.

He pulled back. "You said this Sludic creature caught you. So he knows how to catch you?"

She nodded. "If he uses methods that the Auld consider unethical. Since he started hunting me his ethics have worn rather thin!"

"After he caught you," persisted Peter, "you told him that you wanted to stay here on Earth? That you wouldn't make a nuisance of yourself anymore?"

"I promised to be a good girl from now on if he'd just leave me alone."

"And he refused?"

"He said he was sorry, but it was his duty to arrest me. And, if necessary, to execute me."

"His duty! The bastard! But why? When you've just been annoying them? You never gave away any of their precious secrets." Peter hesitated. "Or did you?"

"No. And I was ready to promise I never would."

"He didn't believe you?"

"He believed that I meant what I said—then! But either I was human or I was not human. If I was not human I was a liar for pretending to be. If I was human, then I'd be as changeable as Earth's weather and belong to a race of convincing liars. Therefore—human or not—I was a liar already!" She laughed. "Trapped in a classical paradox. The kind of paradox that sends your best thinkers running around in circles!"

"Them!" said Peter, with the contempt of the classicist for all current philosophers. "That's the fallacy of the—"

"Darling—Sludic has lots of evidence to show that all men are liars—and women are as bad. Perhaps worse! It's the weak who have to lie and deceive. A survival trait. That's how I managed to survive. Why I'm here now."

"Thank the gods you are!" He hugged her, aching to protect her from danger that could fall from the air. "Why are those Directors so uptight about you?"

"Think, Peter! I know about natural rifts. Something the Auld have kept hidden from all other civilized races. I can fake my way into Transits. I can speak Auld and pass as one. Nobody from any other race can do that. Has ever conceived of doing it! I know—" She hesitated. "Peter—you'll forget all this. As you did before. As you forgot what I told you on the boat."

"I'll never forget you!"

"No—I'm afraid you won't." She sighed. "Some memories are too strong to wipe. But for your own safety you must let me wipe much of what I've said. I know—"

"Darling, you know a hell of a lot. But all you've done is to fool around and annoy. Thalia—a Grace and a Muse. Beautiful and amusing! Don't the Auld have any sense of humor? If they enjoy poetry they must have some. Why do you scare them?"

"Because I'm not to be trusted—as Sludic said so plainly." She bit her lip. "There've been moments when I was so angry, so frustrated, even—yes—so ambitious that I've come close to blowing the whistle on Sludic and his gang of Guards. One day I might really go paranoid and try for revenge. Or get so bored I'd cause chaos for my own amusement! The Muse of Comedy! The Muse of the pratfall! That's classical Greek comedy! Peter, I'm telling you all this—even though you'll forget it— because not telling anybody has sometimes driven me close to telling everybody." She bit her lip again. "Sada's seen the trouble I've left behind. Oh no, nothing dramatic—not so far! Just the silly jokes of a frustrated girl. Not always kind jokes."

"But not malicious! Darling, I know you're not malicious!"

She shifted in his arms. "Sada's nightmare is having thousands of humans loose in the system. Traveling, not for the sport of dodging the Guards or playing puerile pranks to show how much smarter they are than the Auld. Humans without even my weak conscience. Humans traveling under the old drives. Traveling to grab power and loot."

"Power and loot! How the hell can we grab either when we're up against the Guard's blasters?"

"The Guard, Peter, are spread very thin. Very thin indeed. Almost every civilized race in the Arm has surrendered responsibility for its protection to the Guard. The other Arm races are very civilized. Very old and rich. Their survival drives are almost bred out. They're about as ferocious as spayed tabbies now. Even those who were once as tough as the Auld have grown timid with time. The average number of Transit Guards on a civilized world is about fifty, and minor policing is all they ever have to do."

"But fifty Guards with blasters—"

"Peter, I know how to get blasters! If I, alone, suddenly raided any Transit Station on those worlds I could probably hold it long enough to loot. And if I've been tempted to do something very like that, how well do you think Hermann, or Harry, or Rosie—or Pirenne— would resist temptation? What do you think some of those old generals or young activists would do if they were loose in the Transit system with blasters?" She paused. "I told Sludic that I didn't want the Auld to pull out—or let humans in! Not yet?"

"You'd go along with that alien? The animal who's been hunting you?" He stared at her. "What did he say?"

"That he was glad I approved of Transit policy. That he'd always assumed I was intelligent as well as mischievous. No—I don't think he was being sarcastic. Sarcasm's not an Auld trait. One of the things that makes them so boring! He said my approval of the policy would ease his conscience if he had to execute me!"

Peter looked up at the paling sky, trying to think of some way to rescue his love from her nemesis. "That lawyer of yours—Katina Plastiras—she admires you. She'll help you. She'll know all the legal angles." His forehead wrinkled. "She's quite a woman. I've seen her somewhere. Before she contacted me about your money. I can't remember—"

"Don't try! Concentrate on me!"

"But—"

"Katina's brilliant. But U.S. law won't stop Sludic. And he's got the law on his side. The Treaty gives the Auld absolute authority over anybody of any race who uses the Transits. And I've sure used them!" She laughed, and pulled him back to her. "Forget Sludic and Katina for now. Let's use the precious present!"

He gave up trying to place Katina and went back to Thalia's arms. Her story might be crazy, or it might be true, but either way it had removed his fear of her. Whatever she had done, wherever she had been, she was no goddess. It was safe for him to love her.

They fell apart at the first flush of dawn. "Peter! You're superb! But that had better be it, for now!" As the flush spread up into the night sky from the Eastern sea, Thalia jumped to her feet and stood naked, saluting the new day with Sappho's ode. Peter lay entranced, carried upward by the glory of the words and the beauty of the woman.

She finished singing, dropped her arms, and bent to sort out her clothes from Peter's. Then she suddenly paused, bending, something in her hand.

"What's wrong?" Peter crawled from his sleeping bag.

Instead of answering she put a finger to her lips and picked up the locket he had taken off with his clothes, studied it for a moment, then walked quietly across the promontory to set it on a stone near the edge of the cliff. Still signaling him to silence, she returned to Peter and asked in a low voice. "Where did you get that?"

"From you, of course. I hardly ever take it

off. But last night, well, I thought it would get in the way."

She pulled on her jumpsuit, zipped it closed, and faced him. "Peter, that thing's a transponder!"

"What? But you sent it. It has a lock of your hair in it. And your picture!"

"I didn't send it. And that's not a lock of my hair. It's a bunch of fine wires curled to look like hair. The picture's one that Sludic took of me. He sent it!"

"Sludic sent it? But why—?" He stopped as he saw why. "He's been tracking me! In the hope—? Oh God, but I never planned—"

"He reasoned that if he followed you, he'd find me! Sludic's learning about humans! Maybe he's even learning about love!" She glanced up at the sky. "I knew he'd be coming—but not so soon."

"You knew—?"

"I told you he'd be coming!" Thalia showed a trace of irritation. "I left a trail for him to follow. But not so fast! Didn't expect him to arrive for hours yet." Again she looked at the sky. "His ship's up there now."

"He's been tracking me?"

"Tracking you and listening to us. That locket's not just a homing beacon. It's a bug as well. He's been keeping remote tabs on you from the moment you put it on. And he probably heard us making love—and me telling you my story. It was near our heads all night!" She cursed in some unknown language. "He knows you're here. He knows I'm here. And now he knows more about me than I'd want him to know!"

"Darling, I'm sorry—"

"It's not your fault. It's mine. Sludic gets a bit smarter every time we tangle. And I get a bit dumber! His ship's on its way down. My guess is that he'll arrive with full daylight."

"Why doesn't he come now?"

"Precipitate action isn't an Auld characteristic. Cover all angles first is their way. Not a bad way!" She looked at Peter with affectionate concern, then went softly across the promontory and came back with the locket, motioning him to silence. When he started to speak she clapped a hand over his mouth. "Peter, you've got to forget! Sada's sworn not to harm you. But—from the way he's been acting lately—if he thinks you're a danger to the Transits he might do the unthinkable and break his oath!" She was holding the locket up, as if she wanted her every word to be carried clearly. "Forget—as you did on the ferry!" Her fingers slid from his mouth to his forehead. "After I've gone you'll remember me, but everything I've told you about the Auld and the Transits and the Arm—that'll be only a confused dream!"

He took her fingers and kissed the tips. "It's a confused dream already. And now I'm sure you're a goddess!"

She smiled sadly and put the locket down on the grass. Then she went into rapid action, packing her gear, pulling on her combat coveralls, tightening the chin-strap of her helmet, checking her weapons. Peter began to dress and pack his own gear.

She settled her harness, moved to stand over the locket, and shouted, "Peter—there's an Auld ship coming! I can sense it!"

"How—? Why—?"

"How can I shoot it down? I haven't got a blaster?"

He gaped at her. He didn't know what a blaster looked like but the weapon at her hip, the other weapon she had stowed in her pack, they both fitted his picture of blasters.

She saw his confusion and smiled. The smile of a Thalia preparing some bitter comedy. A smile that made Peter shiver and revived his dormant fear of this woman. Then she looked past him, toward the entrance of a ravine at the top of the scree, a ravine running back into the mountain. A goat had wandered out to breakfast on the thorny underbrush. She gestured him to silence, drew the weapon at her hip, and aimed. The goat dropped.

He stared, aghast. "Thalia! You didn't have to kill—"

"Shut up!" A glance of irritated affection. She walked softly back to the locket, picked it up, and whispered a few words of Greek, words he did not catch. Again she smiled her Thalian smile and called, "I must get airborne before Sludic arrives!"

"I'll stop him!"

"You stay here! Sada won't harm you. He swore an oath he wouldn't harm you. He won't break his word. And you're the poet he admires!" She looked up at the sky, as though challenging her invisibile enemy. Then she looked down at the grass and saw her panties. "Damn! Forgot those!" She slipped the locket into a pouch and picked them up. "No time to put these on now!" She tossed them to Peter. "Have these as a keepsake! Underwear of a goddess."

He caught them. "I'm damned if I'll stay behind while you're being hunted! What do you think I am?"

"A brave poet!" She grabbed him, gave him a hard-mouthed kiss. "Send your songs to the stars!" Then she went scrambling up the scree toward the fallen goat, her blaster in her hand.

Peter stared up at the sky, looked at her panties, flung them down onto the grass, and started up the scree after her.

XV

"She's heading for her aircraft." Sludic stood up. "We'll catch her in the air and knock her into the sea. A clean death." He started toward the flightdeck.

"No!" Katina ran after him, caught his arm. "I'm your conscience! Remember? You mustn't kill her. You promised!"

Bose stayed staring at the tracker, listening to the loudspeaker. On the screen a bright dot marked the position of the bug on the island below. From the speaker came the whisper of the wind and the rustle of the grass; Alia's cry still echoed in his ears. "I must get airborne before Sludic arrives!"

His ship had arrived. The Marshal and his

squad of Transit Guards were poised high above Psara, preparing to go down and take the fugitive they had hunted so long. They had hovered above the island all night, listening to the murmured voices of the lovers, hearing Alia tell Peter her story. Now it was dawn and her story was about to end.

Quine's report had reached Sludic the day after he had impressed Bose and Katina into his squad. "The suspect calling herself Ruth Adams was photographed at Dulles Airport boarding an airliner for Athens at 1723 hours on 28th March." The squad had scrambled; within hours Sludic's ship had been over Greece. By then the trail was two days old and already lost. Alia had arrived at Hellenicon Airport, exchanged greetings with the man she had knocked out, gently refused his invitation to dinner, and disappeared into the city.

The Marshal had been furious. Not only had the fugitive evaded him once again, Quine's report had reached others besides himself. Terran agencies which had given up the chase after learning that Alia had left Earth, had returned to the hunt. Sludic had become obsessed with catching or killing her before his human competitors grabbed his quarry, before they extracted her story. And hearing her full story via the bug he had planted on Peter had hardened his obsession into an almost human callousness.

They had been flying over the Aegean for a week—the Auld ship required neither refueling nor servicing. It drew its energy from the angular inertia of the rotating Galaxy, the same inexhaustible source which powered most Auld machines, from the Transit engines which shot cargoes between worlds to blasters which focused that energy into beams which stunned or destroyed.

The ship flew at supersonic speeds close to the edge of space and was large enough for some forty Guards and two humans to live aboard in fair comfort. "I'll bet we're the first humans to fly in one of these things!" Katina had said, and then had concentrated on learning all she could about the ship while she had the chance. Until the moment they had picked up Alia's voice on the bug she had been confident that Alia would never be caught. She no longer seemed confident. Even after the Marshal had shaken her off she had followed him onto the flightdeck, interrupting the orders he was giving the pilot, crying, "You mustn't kill her! You'll suffer too much if you do!"

Bose had seen death on Sludic's face from the moment they learned that Alia had disappeared in Athens. He had been too depressed to take much interest in the ship. And Katina had been wrong; they were not the first humans to fly in an Auld ship. He had flown in one twenty years before. Now, as then, it was an example of Auld technological superiority. Humans would never catch up. It was futile to try. Alia could not evade all the forces against her. At first he had hoped that Sludic would catch her before some human agency did. Now he knew that all outcomes of the hunt would end the same way.

They had followed Peter's meanderings among the Greek islands. Katina had fired Sludic's fury at the speed with which Quine's report had leaked through Unipol to other Terran agencies, by reminding him that she and Doctor Bose had advised against leaving Quine with a free hand. Sludic's reaction had verged on violence. After seeing it, Bose had not dared to accuse the Marshal of lying in act if not in words by planting a bug on the man he had sworn not to harm. When Sludic had admitted the bug was a locket containing a picture of Alia and some purported hair, he had come close to impugning the Marshal's honor. But this was getting more and more like a Terran police operation, and in such operations truthfulness and honor are not major considerations.

Sludic had also started to show human guile. His reading of Terran romances had convinced the Marshal that the two lovers planned to meet; that was why Peter was wandering between islands and why Alia had flown to Athens. Bose had had a foreboding that Sludic might be right when Peter had landed on Psara the previous afternoon. "Psara?" the Marshal had said. "Is not that the island where they first met?"

Bose had nodded. Katina had bitten her lip. All three of them had crowded round the tracker in the after compartment of the ship, waiting to see if Alia would indeed come. With darkness the ship had dropped down until they were hovering at ten thousand meters and the outline of the island had filled the screen. Below them Peter had fallen asleep, still alone. Perhaps, after all, this was a wild goose chase. Perhaps only chance or sentiment had brought him back to Psara on this anniversary. Perhaps there was no rendezvous.

That hope had been blasted an hour before midnight. A Guard had come aft, speaking the English the Auld always used when humans were present. "There's an aircraft approaching the island from the direction of Chios. The radar signal suggests it's a minicopter."

"If it lands near him—then it's her!" Sludic had gone for'rd to watch the radar. He had returned in sad triumph. "It's landed only a kilometer away. Somewhere on the side of the mountain. Who but Alia would land in darkness on a mountainside?"

Because Auld night-vision was poor they avoided night actions. Bose had remembered that from his first contact with them twenty years before. But it was not going to help Alia, flying into the trap. Sludic had only to hover above the island and capture her at dawn.

Muffled voices had started to come from the locket. "She's arrived!" Sludic had said. "The range is so short that when he takes off his clothes we'll be able to hear what they say to each other."

They had heard. They had sat listening to the bug repeating the surprise of the lovers at finding each other again, and then to their endearments. To Peter telling Thalia why he was on the island. Chance and sentiment—not some prearranged plan—had brought the lovers together. Lovers now happy in their love, unconscious of fate hanging high above them.

They had heard Alia telling her story, claiming to have been born on this very island two thousand four hundred years ago, falling through a natural transit, wandering among savage worlds with a war party on the far rim of the Arm. With every revelation Sludic had looked grimmer. When she had described a network of natural transits he had cursed in Auld. She had condemned Peter and herself to death.

She had knowledge too dangerous to know. Bose doubted that he and Katina would survive. He was certain they would never be allowed to return to Earth. Sludic might now look and talk like a human; he was still essentially Auld. And the Auld put the well-being of the many above fairness to the few. Duty was all. The security of the Transits above everything. As Alia had hinted to Peter, as Bose was seeing for himself, the Marshal had acquired an element of ruthlessness and duplicity along with his facade of humanity. To defend the Transits against intrusion he would kill his best friend as surely as he would kill his worst enemy. He would suffer for both killings afterward but his duty would prevent him from sparing either.

After the lovers had fallen asleep Bose had sat huddled while the ship hovered, waiting for the dawn to let the hunters go in and take their quarry. The woman who had once been a human girl and the poet who was all too human. Katina, bending beside him, had whispered, "We've got to help them!"

Bose had shrugged and said nothing. He had had nothing to suggest. They were in combat gear but armed only with pistols, useless against coveralls, while the Guards had blasters. He sat by the tracker, looking like the aliens who came and went through the after compartment, detesting what they were about to do.

It's easier for Katina, Bose had thought. She has only one loyalty now—to Thalia. His own was split. Sludic had been right all along. Thalia was too dangerous to roam free. The knowledge of a natural transit would rouse in the human race all the old savage ambitions and set them searching for the other rifts which must certainly exist. The worst of humanity would spew out across the Arm if men heard there were rich worlds which could be reached and plundered. Until humans were prepared to join Arm civilization on civilized terms they must be caged.

But the animal within him was already howling defiance at these aliens who presumed to cage it. The part of every human which had kept a cowed silence when the bars of the cage had appeared unbreakable, when the Auld were believed to be invincible. The barbarian in every man which would rise to shake loose the bars if it learned that the bars could be broken, that the Auld were not invincible. When it realized the Transit Guard was spread thinly over a multitude of wealthy worlds inhabited by soft-shelled peoples. The human hunger for freedom and the barbarian lust for loot could drive men out across the Arm as they had driven the Golden Horde out of the deserts. In what captured city had some unlucky woman been raped so he, Alexander Selin Tanaka Bose, could have a share in her genes?

The tracker had come alive again when the lovers woke and he had had to listen to their whispered endearments until they had moved out of range of the bug. Then there had been a few soft words in Greek which had meant something to Katina but nothing to him. Nor to Sludic.

They had heard Alia cry, "I must get airborne before Sludic arrives!" Then, a moment later, "I haven't got a blaster!" That was when Sludic had gone forward, ordering the pilot to shoot her down when the minicopter rose from the darkness of the ravine into the dawn sunlight.

Katina was still protesting. "Capture her alive! I'm your conscience. That's why you brought us."

"My conscience tells me to kill her cleanly in the air. My conscience will not let me risk the life of my Guards."

"Shoot down an unarmed woman? What risk is there to your Guards in trying to take her on the ground? You heard her tell Peter she hasn't got a blaster." Katina caught the Marshal by the arm, pulled him back to the monitor, and hit the replay stud. "Listen!"

Reluctantly Sludic listened. Again he heard

Alia saying, "I haven't got a blaster!" He pressed his fingertips to his eyes and seemed entirely human, a weary human torn by doubts and emotions. After a moment he said, "Alex, Katina, if I try to capture Alia alive this one more time, will you help me?"

"Of course! I swear!" said Katina.

"Alex—you too?"

"Sada—I don't know."

"Alex's UN. He's a vacillator!" Katina interrupted. "Alia won't listen to him anyway. But she'll listen to me. I've saved her life once already."

Sludic did not answer, but called to the pilot, "Land near those pillars."

The ship dropped through the dawn sunlight, shot under the shadow of the mountain, and landed on the promontory near the ruined temple. Sludic jumped to the ground, his blaster drawn, waving his Guards back. The only sign of the lovers was the flattened grass in the hollow where they had made love.

"Her aircraft must be hidden in one of those ravines." Sludic reached back into the ship for a hand tracker, swung it, and took a reading. "They're up that ravine to the left—about five hundred meters." He watched the dot on the miniature screen. "Moving slowly and irregularly. Exhausted from climbing that scree. Or perhaps one of them's hurt."

"Give them a chance to surrender!" Katina dropped down beside him.

"I will if we can catch her before she takes off." He rechecked the tracker, then called to his pilot. "Land on the mountain near the head of that valley. Section One—spread out along the lip of the ravine. Stun anyone you see moving below. Section Two—stay by the ship, ready to go down into the ravine after her. All of you—if she reaches her aircraft, stun her as she takes off. Whatever her altitude!" He paused, listening to the acknowledgment of his orders.

He's giving them in English, so we can understand, thought Bose. Decent of him. Or to show them his determination?

"Pilot!" the Marshal continued. "If she rises out of the ravine—take off and ram her! Do not hesitate!"

The pilot raised his hand in acknowledgment. Had he ever killed anybody? Had any of the Squad ever killed before? Had Sludic? The Marshal was looking at him. "Alex, if you want to save us from that—come with me!"

"That's your UN job, isn't it, Doctor Bose?" taunted Katina. "Saving Auld sensitivities! Saving them from having to kill us humans?"

In a way it was. Even in this disastrous situation. He lowered himself slowly through the hatch and went to stand with Sludic and

Katina. The Marshal signaled his ship to take off and they watched it swerve up toward the mountain. The ravine would be ringed by Guards long before Alia could reach her mini-copter. If she did reach it and tried to escape by air she would be blasted out of it or rammed into the sea.

Bose turned and saw a flash of white on the grass near the base of one of the pillars. Sludic saw it too and went to pick it up. "Her underwear! They must have left in a hurry. How did she sense my ship was coming?" He shook his head and dropped the panties.

We interrupted them making love, thought Bose, sick with shame. Alia, like a salmon, had come home to mate. And, like a salmon, she would be trapped and die because of her mating. "Sada—if they surrender, how will they live?"

"Peter Ward—under light restrictions. Alia—under more rigorous constraints. If they fail to surrender, I'll try to stun them. I don't want to kill either of them. But if they're escaping—or if any of my Guard are in danger—then I'll kill them both." He paused. "Alex—do you understand?"

Bose nodded. Sludic was showing a measure of gallantry. Going after Alia himself with only two conscripted humans as allies. Gallantry—or the need to prove that a single Auld was more than a match for any human, even one with Alia's skills?

"Good! Then follow me!" The words of an officer going into action. The Marshal turned, ran across the open ground, and started to scramble up the scree toward the entrance of the ravine to the left, the tracker in one hand, his blaster in the other. Katina, her faceplate down, her pistol drawn, ran after him.

Bose began by running, but the slope was steep, the scree was loose, he was forty, and even Katina could not keep up the pace set by Sludic. The Marshal disappeared into the ravine's entrance a full thirty seconds before she had gained the foot of the cliffs. Bose had to slow to a walk when he was only halfway up the slope, and arrived panting to lean against the rocks, recover his wind, and gather his resolution.

After a couple of minutes he had regained sufficient breath and resolve to plunge into the ravine after her. The going was rough and the sweat was pouring down over his eyes so that he could hardly see with his face-plate closed. He was staring at the ground when he reached the first bend. He stumbled around it and almost ran into Katina's back.

"What—?" he began, then realized she had her arms above her head. An instant later his own were up too. Facing them was Peter with a gun in his hand and a look which showed he was eager to use it.

"Thalia!" Peter called over his shoulder. "I've got 'em both! The bitch from the FBI and the alien-loving doc." Then he lowered his voice and spat, "Why couldn't you leave her alone? Why can't you let us live in peace? Katina, you know the score! Why are you fronting for those devils?"

"Professor Ward," said Katina, speaking calmly despite the pistol pointing at her stomach, "You can't get away. Give yourself up before Sludic has an excuse to blast you. You saw his ship. His whole squad will be here in seconds."

"I can hold 'em long enough for Thalia to escape!"

But how? thought Bose. That pistol can't penetrate a combat suit. It couldn't penetrate Katina's suit. Nor his. So why was she standing with her arms above her head? Why was he? But he kept his own up, uncertain what to do.

Thalia appeared, suddenly and silently from a vine-covered cleft behind Peter and darted a quick glance at Katina, who gave a slight nod. Then she called, "Peter!"

Startled, the young man turned his head and the edge of Katina's hand struck the side of his neck. He collapsed where he stood. Bose suddenly realized that Thalia had a blaster pointing at him. The next moment he subsided slowly to the ground. The muscles of his larynx were too weak for him to protest: it was a struggle to continue breathing, to keep his eyes open. He thought, *She had a blaster. So she lied. And Sada believed her!*

Thalia came to stand above him, looking down at him. "Sorry I had to do that, Alex. You can still breathe? Good! Don't try to talk. It's a mild curare-like effect. Paralysis of voluntary muscles. Only temporary." She turned to Katina who was kneeling beside Peter. "How long will he stay out?"

"About fifteen minutes." Katina spoke and acted with the assurance of the expert. She rolled the unconscious man onto his stomach, turned his head to one side, made sure his breathing was not obstructed. "He'll wake up like your suitor in Athens. Sore neck and broken heart!"

Thalia laughed. "When he recovers treat him like a hero."

"He is a hero!" She ruffled the young man's hair. "He's just not very efficient."

"Look after him. Please! He needs looking after."

"I will. I promise." She glanced at the ravine. "Though if you can't handle Sludic we'll all need looking after."

"I'll nail Sada. When he catches that goat

and comes roaring back he'll find you've got Peter. Tell him that you've cornered both of us. That Alex has me hammerlocked in a cave back there, and doesn't dare move until he gets help!" Thalia knelt and kissed Peter's forehead. "Good-bye, my sweet poet. Write a sonnet that will make me immortal." She squeezed Katina's shoulder, and then came to stand over Bose, who had been listening incredulously to the conversation. Peter was right. She had the classical characteristics of a goddess. Beautiful, cruel, proud, passionate, and capricious.

Also considerable strength. She reached down and pulled him to his feet. "Alex, your muscles should be strong enough to move you, if I help. So move this way!" She propelled him ahead of her through the curtain of vines, along an overgrown defile, and into a dimly lit cave where she seated him on a rock. "Stay there!"

He had to obey for he could not yet move without aid. But enough strength had returned to the muscles of his larynx for him to gasp an accusation. "Katina—she's betrayed me! And you—you've betrayed Peter!"

"Katina hasn't betrayed you. And I haven't betrayed Peter. I've saved Peter. Both his life and his ego. If I'd taken him where I'm going he'd be dead within days. Me too probably— killed trying to protect him. He's full of heroic enthusiasm but he forgot that a bullet won't penetrate a combat suit. Peter's a good poet. He may even be great. But half his mind's away on Parnassus most of the time. He acts on romantic impulse. Love and beauty divert him. You saw what he did when I called his name. He forgot he was covering my escape, turned his head, and Katina took him in one!"

"So he's humiliated—"

"Humiliated? No way! When he wakes up and finds I'm gone Katina'll tell him that I only escaped because of his self-sacrifice. And, in a way, that's true. Peter's heroic but he's a romantic—and there's no romance where I'm going. I plan to get Sada!"

"If you kill Sada—"

"I'm not going to kill Sada unless he makes me. I want him alive, armed, and willing. I'm taking the natural transit. This is the cave. I don't have to wait for the stars." She hefted her blaster. "One full blast will open it. That's what I was saying when I switched to Greek—for Katina's benefit. She phoned me when Sada ordered her and you to the Terminal. I knew he planned to force you both to join the hunt. I laid a trail to bring him here. I didn't plan for Peter to come too! When I found that bugged locket I hoped she'd be listening. She was—and got the message. She saw what I was up to as soon as Peter appeared. Katina's very smart!"

"She's a faithless little bitch with the worst of your talents!" Bose tried to struggle to his feet and failed. "What do you mean, 'get Sada'?"

"Persuade Sada to come with me. I've a rough trip ahead and my chances of getting through are quadrupled if Sada's guarding my back. He'd better! Because if I'm killed there'll be nobody to guard his."

"The Transit Authority will make Earth pay—"

"The Directors don't know Sada's back on Earth. They seldom know where he is. He's a high-level independent—a free lance. One of the few Auld capable of acting independently. His sense of duty is enough to keep him faithful to Auld ideals. The security of the Transits is his only aim. God, what a prig! As for me— they think I'm safely on Larga, filing stacks of data. I'd rather be in Hell." She brooded a moment. "So if Sada and I disappear together they'll assume that I was killed trying to escape and he was killed in the line of duty. Nobody'll know what happened."

"Peter'll know. I'll know. Katina will know."

"Peter'll say it all in verse, which humans won't read and aliens will enjoy but won't understand. You're Sada's friend, so you'll do nothing to shame him. Your duty-sense is almost as constricting as an Auld's. Katina will know, but she'll also know what to do with the knowledge. She won't broadcast it. Katina has ideas."

"She and you—a pair of—" He stopped, not for fear of her but because he couldn't find words to exactly describe his feelings about either of them. "Where's Sada now?" His muscles were recovering some of their strength, but he remained limp and apparently helpless.

"He passed us about five hundred meters astern of a goat with the locket hanging from its neck. One dirty trick deserves another. Giving poor Peter a bugged picture of me indeed!" She scowled, then laughed. "Sada should be coming back soon in a pure Auld fury. And therefore not thinking too clearly."

As if on cue there was a rustle in the underbrush outside the cave and Katina appeared in the entrance. "I can hear Sludic crashing toward us." She saw Bose's expression. "Don't worry, Alex! Just hang loose. This is a stake-out where the hunter's snared and the bait's unharmed. I'll justify everything to you when it's all over."

Thalia went to the mouth of the cave and caught Katina in her arms. "Don't push too hard!"

Katina hugged her. "I'll block my urge to act the idiot. And you—you stop poking the hill just to upset the ants!" The two women kissed and then Katina was gone.

Minutes later Sludic's curse came from the ravine. It sounded as if he had charged around a corner, fallen over Peter, and then seen Katina. "You've got him? Good! Where's Alex?"

"Up that cleft. Sitting on Alia. We jumped them both. He's waiting for you to take over. Go and bring her out." Katina's voice rose an octave as Sludic started toward the defile. "For God's sake, be careful!"

The little liar! thought Bose furiously, unable to shout because of Thalia's hand over his mouth. Not only had Katina's training made her an expert in deception, she had told the Marshal what he had been longing to hear.

He came along the defile, making a lot of noise as he moved. Scouting through close cover was evidently not among his skills. When he arrived at the mouth of the cave he stood staring into the shadows, saw Thalia apparently trying to break away from Bose. Shouting, "Hold her, Alex!" he charged into the cave. Then he saw her blaster and stopped dead.

"You hold it, Sada!" Thalia was still embracing Bose. "We're in a natural transit. A blast'll rupture the boundaries. All three will be sucked in together. But we'll come out separately—God knows where!"

"What have you done to Alex?" Sludic's eyes had adjusted and he had seen the expression on Bose's face.

"Mild muscular paralysis. No harm and he's recovering fast."

"Let him go! Get him out of danger." Sludic hesitated, "Let Alex go and I'll let you escape!" He choked over the words.

"You'll let me escape? Thanks! I could have skipped any time. But I don't relish making a second trip solo. I only got through last time because I was small and skinny. They made me into a pet instead of a meal. Now—I'm too big to pet but the right size for the pot."

"Alia—what do you want."

"You! And a truce till we reach civilization again. I want you to come with me down this transit. Together we might make it. With two blasters we could cover each other. With two of us we'll get some sleep."

"Why didn't you take Peter?"

"Because Peter's brave, inquisitive, moral, generous, and self-sacrificing. He's also a dreamer. Any combination of those is lethal where I'm going." She paused, then went on. "If you won't come with me, I'll have to take Alex. His reactions are right. He'll be good in a crunch. Perhaps better than you, Sada. Alex doesn't jump to convictions and follow them to the end. He wouldn't have followed that goat with the locket!" She laughed and Sludic winced. "Also, I'll have a lover. At least at the start."

"Alia—I can't betray the Transits. And Alex—he's my friend!"

"You're lucky to have a friend. All I've got is an enemy—you!"

Her voice faltered and Bose was shaken by impotent fury as he heard her using him like a betting chip in a bluff. She was bluffing; she hadn't the brutal fiber to carry her bluff through. She'd go alone rather than take an unwilling companion. She hadn't the determination to destroy Sada by forcing him to choose between friendship and duty.

When she'd said "I'll have a lover" his spasm of desire had been stronger than any he had ever felt, even during his hot hungers as a young man. And she had fanned another dying ember. Her description of the new and dangerous worlds to be crossed, the strange things to be seen, had sounded like the kind of call he had heard and answered when, as a young doctor, he had set out to struggle against dirt, disease, and death. When he had been driven by a hunger for excitement as well as by a need to do good.

His vision of passionate love and high adventure was slipping away as Sludic stood torn apart by his choice, as Thalia showed she was too soft to make it. A pair of pussycats pretending to be tigers! She'd leave them both, go alone to her probable death. Leaving him to live on as a bruised buffer between humans and aliens.

The two old enemies were staring at each other. A face-off to decide the survival of Thalia's body or Sada's psyche. Their preoccupation with themselves and with their own ethics fired his rage. A rage which flooded his body with adrenalin, brought back strength to his muscles. He was the only real human there.

Sludic and Thalia were now mesmerized by their own emotions, by this end to a hunt which had lasted for millennia and taken them both across the Arm. They were locked in the bonds which form between hunter and hunted; now they were finding how tightly those bonds held them. They stood, blasters loose in their hands, as their eyes explored each other's faces.

Bose estimated distances and then exploded. His foot caught Sludic's blaster and sent it spinning across the cave. His right hand twisted Thalia's from her grasp. His jump, flowing directly from his kick, spun him around. He finished with his back against the wall, with her blaster holding both Sludic and Thalia in its beam.

They stared at him, thunderstruck; as amazed as if the rock on which he had been sitting had attacked them. Before either could move he snapped, "Dead still both of you! Or I'll open the channel and we'll each go separately." He steadied, and took a deep breath. "You've lost your options. You've only two alternatives. Do we go as a group? Or do we go alone?"

Thalia recovered first. "Alex—do you want to go?"

"Want to head out across the Arm with a half-human alien and a dehumanized woman? At my age? Of course not! But I want to stay here even less. I wouldn't trust either of you alone with each other."

"Alex, you don't have to take the responsibility—" Sludic started to say.

"Sada, you Auld have been taking other peoples' responsibilities for eons. And a miserable, unimaginative, guilt-racked race it's turned you into. You know that! And that's why you've started to bring humans into the Transit Administration. But you're moving too slowly. Alia was right when she said the Transit situation's becoming critical. So that's why it's better if all three of us are out of circulation for a while."

"But there aren't any humans in the Transit Administration. Not yet."

"There's one. A human time-bomb, primed by Thalia. A time-bomb named Katina Plastiras. She's one reason why all three of us have to go. If we stay you'll try to block her, Thalia and I'll try to help her. She mustn't be hampered by us. Cheer up, Sada! Overwhelming force cleans even an Auld conscience. Thalia, how do we make sure we stay together?"

She was staring at him, her blue eyes bright with anger, admiration, and interest. "Alex, let me get my pack and my spare blaster first. No tricks—I swear!"

A liar to the last? But her look made him believe her. "Get it!"

She moved across the cave, fished a blaster from her pack, snapped the pack onto her harness, and returned to stand between him and Sludic. "Stay together? We huddle, facing inward. Grab each other tight. Like this!" She put one arm around the Marshal, the other around Bose. "Hang onto me and each other. Remember, when we land—if we land—we'll be facing inward. So turn immediately, blaster set at full. God knows what we'll be landing among! Whatever it is, don't wait to ask. If it makes a move toward us—shoot! Ready everyone? Alex—tell me when I'm to spring the action!"

They hugged each other, waiting for Bose to speak. Thalia started laughing.

"What's so funny?" Bose demanded. He was beginning to appreciate the enormity of his decision and to wonder if he was being wise.

"Sada once asked me why I came to Earth. I told him I came to get what I wanted. I didn't tell him I didn't know what that was. Now I do. And you two are roughly it." She saw Bose starting to speak. "Hang on tight, boys! Here we go!"

Her blaster flashed. There was a sharp implosion. Then Thalia, Bose, and Sludic, clutching each other, began falling across the Arm toward a savage world without a name.

DAW

JO CLAYTON

"Aleytys is a heroine as tough as, and more believable and engaging than, the general run of swords-and-sorcery barbarians."

—*Publishers Weekly*

The saga of Aleytys is recounted in these DAW books:

☐ **DIADEM FROM THE STARS** (#UE1977—$2.50)

☐ **LAMARCHOS** (#UE1627—$2.25)

☐ **IRSUD** (#UE1839—$2.50)

☐ **MAEVE** (#UE1760—$2.25)

☐ **STAR HUNTERS** (#UE1871—$2.50)

☐ **THE NOWHERE HUNT** (#UE1874—$2.50)

☐ **GHOSTHUNT** (#UE1823—$2.50)

☐ **THE SNARES OF IBEX** (#UE1974—$2.75)*

* Nov. 1984

The Duel of Sorcerers Series

☐ **MOONGATHER** (#UE1729—$2.95)

☐ **MOONSCATTER** (#UE1798—$2.95)

☐ **CHANGER'S MOON** (Forthcoming, 1985)

NEW AMERICAN LIBRARY,
P.O. Box 999, Bergenfield, New Jersey 07621

Please send me the DAW BOOKS I have checked above. I am enclosing
$_____ (check or money order—no currency or C.O.D.'s).
Please include the list price plus $1.00 per order to cover handling costs.

Name _____

Address _____

City _____ State _____ Zip Code _____
Please allow at least 4 weeks for delivery

DAW

A GALAXY OF SCIENCE FICTION STARS!